S0-EAR-579

"So, the question on everybody's lips these days is why would Khaled, the best-selling voice in the game, retire so suddenly?"

Khaled looked into the television screen. He had cut his curls, and looked even better than before as a result. Jessica clutched a pillow closely and listened intently. Just a few short weeks ago, she had been devastated to hear of Khaled's retirement.

"I decided to go back to school. Education is important you know. I want this to be an example, especially to my young fans."

"Oh, my," Jessica breathed. "He believes in education."

Clay straightened up in his seat. What was Khaled up to? He wished he could see his face and how he answered the questions.

The interviewer looked bemused. "You are a multimillionaire. Why go back to school?"

"It's something I've always wanted to do, and now it seems like as good time as any. I have six albums under my belt. I have been doing this for years now. I am just taking a hiatus. Maybe when I go back to school I will be inspired, write new material, and come back fresh for the seventh album."

JUST TO SEE HER

BRENDA BARRETT

JAMAICA
TREASURES

JUST TO SEE HER

Published by Jamaica Treasures
Kingston, Jamaica

This is a work of fiction. Names, characters, places, and incidents are either the product of the author's imagination or are used fictitiously. Any resemblance to an actual person or persons, living or dead, events, or locales is entirely coincidental.

All rights reserved
Copyright © 2014 by Brenda Barrett

No part of this book may be reproduced or transmitted in any form or by any means, electronic or mechanical, including photocopying, recording, or by any information storage and retrieval system, without permission in writing from the Publisher, except where permitted by law.

ISBN - 978-976-8247-08-7
Jamaica Treasures Ltd.
P.O. Box 482
Kingston 19
Jamaica W.I.
www.fiwibooks.com

Other books in the Bancroft Family Series:

ALSO BY BRENDA BARRETT

ABOUT THE AUTHOR

Books have always been a big part of life for Jamaican born Brenda Barrett, she reports that she gets withdrawal symptoms if she does not consume at least two books per week. That is all she can manage these days, as her days are filled with writing, a natural progression from her love of reading. Currently, Brenda has several novels on the market, she writes predominantly in the historical fiction, Christian fiction, comedy and romance genres.

Apart from writing fictional books, Brenda writes for her blogs blackhair101.com; where she gives hair care tips and fiwibooks.com, where she shares about her writing life.

You can connect with Brenda online at:
Brenda-Barrett.com
Twitter.com/AuthorWriterBB
Facebook.com/AuthorBrendaBarrett

Chapter One

"I can't believe it," Jessica said, walking into the science lab where her best friend, Ramon, was writing his lab paper.

"What?" Ramon removed his glasses and rubbed his eyes. "Did someone die? You look like you were crying."

"I am devastated." Jessica slumped onto the stool that was in front of Ramon and tried to blink away the tears that were in her eyes. "I am shell-shocked. I can't believe it."

Ramon was quite used to Jessica's melodramatic ways, so he patiently waited to hear about the latest event in her life.

"I just can't process it," Jessica said, bowing her head and shaking it vigorously. "It's like the end of the world, the end of an era, the end of..."

"Just tell me," Ramon gritted out. "I have to finish this lab report."

"Khaled is retiring from music and performing," Jessica said tremulously. "They just announced it on Entertainment News. I heard it while eating lunch, and I couldn't swallow another bite of my turkey burger. It's as if a piece of my heart were ripped from my chest and thrown to the ground, its bloody entrails fluttering as I sat there watching it slowly stopped beating."

Ramon grinned. Not only was Jessica melodramatic but she could be poetic as well.

"I swear my life is over." A tear actually slipped down her cheeks. "I spent three years studying music, hoping that one day I would meet Khaled and write some songs, or produce something for him."

"And you dreamt that you could be with him and have his babies," Ramon said, grinning. "Boo hoo hoo."

He bent over his lab book and continued writing, not an ounce of sympathy for Jessica and her sadness.

"You are supposed to be my best friend," Jessica hiccupped. "I can't stand you!"

She looked around the lab. Two other guys were in the farthest corner; one of them was looking at her sympathetically. He waved when her eyes met his. The other was scribbling fast in a book; he looked like he was writing a lab report as well.

Jessica looked away from the one who was watching her with sympathy in his eyes. She watched his reflection in the glass; he was still staring at her even though she had turned away her head.

She closed her eyes. She couldn't process having a new guy checking her out right now. This must be the worst day of her life to date. Everybody thought that she was a little bit too obsessed with Khaled, and maybe she was, but she loved his music. His music was soulful and profound. His lyrics spoke to her. They had been speaking to her from she was fifteen, and now, at twenty-one, her precious Khaled was retiring. It was as if she were losing her best friend.

There would be no new songs and no more news about him in the media so that she could keep up with what's happening in his life. His retirement devastated her in a way that nobody would understand.

"Hi, I'm Clay." The guy who had been sitting at the other end of the lab was standing in front of her, and she hadn't even noticed. "I couldn't avoid hearing what you said about Khaled. Is it true that he is retiring?"

"Yes," Jessica said miserably. "Are you a Khaled fan too?"

"I guess you could say so. I like his music." Clay looked at her closely. "You are Jessica Bancroft, aren't you?"

"Yes," Jessica nodded. "How'd you know?"

"You have been coming to see Ramon all summer. When you stand at the door, I usually admire your curly golden hair." Clay looked over at Ramon who was steadily working and ignoring them. "I thought you were Ramon's girlfriend."

"Not likely," Jessica scoffed. "He mocks me all the time. I can't even grieve properly without being ignored."

"You act like a teeny bopper, not a grown third-year university student," Ramon said, still studiously looking over his paper. "If I had a girlfriend, she'd have to be mature and...." He held up his head and smirked, "She can't like Khaled. I would prefer if she outright hated his music. I can't stand that twits name; I've had too many years of you talking to me about him. He has a nice voice, and he sings—what's the obsession?" He slapped his lab report in frustration. "Are you done with your lab report?" he asked Clay.

Clay nodded. "I am; it wasn't so hard."

"What were your conclusions?"

Jessica sighed. They were about to talk science. "I am outta here." She grabbed her rucksack, which she had thrown over the top of the desk. "I knew I shouldn't have come in here to share my pain with you, Ramon 'Heartless' Rodriguez."

"Wait, Jessica," Clay said, hurrying to get his books. He handed his lab report to Ramon. "Everything is detailed here. I even gave it a little extra attention. You can give it back to me in tomorrow's Advanced Chem' class."

"Oh, cool." Ramon gratefully took the paper. "Thanks, man." Ramon looked over at Jessica dispassionately. "Bye, Jess. Please call me only when you are done grieving."

Jessica snorted. "You are some friend."

She headed through the door with Clay following in her wake. She hurried up the steps leading to the lobby area on the second floor of the science building while Clay kept pace with her.

"My hair is not golden; it's just light brown," Jessica said when they exited the science building. She had no destination in mind. She had one class later that evening. Her day was wide open and she was feeling down.

Clay stopped beside her.

"You are right; it's light brown with a golden hue. It matches your eyes too. You are pretty."

"Thanks." Jessica shrugged. "I hear that all the time."

"And modest," Clay said, grinning.

"I have never really seen you around here before," Jessica said, looking at Clay as she took off in the direction of the garden in front of the president's building. Maybe a garden setting would be perfect for her now.

"That's because you only have eyes for Ramon." Clay was keeping up with Jessica's long legged strides but almost bumped into her when she slowed down.

"That's ridiculous." Jessica frowned. "I don't have eyes just for Ramon."

"Well, okay then, if you say so." Clay shrugged. "Where are you going?"

"I don't know," Jessica looked confused. "I am going

through a tragedy right now. I need to think. Maybe sit down with all six of Khaled's albums and mourn."

"Ah," Clay shook his head. "You feel that strongly about him retiring? Think of it from his side though: six albums in six years, plus touring must have been hard on him. He needs a break."

"He is just twenty-eight," Jessica said feelingly. "He could quit when he's older. This was sudden and disturbing. What is he going to do now?"

Clay shrugged. "What does a handsome millionaire singer do when he quits? Have a long vacation in some exotic place with lots of naked girls and liquor."

"Not Khaled!" Jessica said vehemently, "not Khaled. He is different. Not once have I ever heard him being linked to any female or going to parties, or anything like that. He's not the typical celebrity."

"Are you kidding?" Clay said, laughing. "Every other month he has a new girl on his arm at some premier or the other."

"That's just it: They are just props for photographs," Jessica said. "In an interview Khaled admitted that his producers required that of him. It is just the business."

Jessica stopped at the garden and sat on one of the three stone benches, which were positioned at scenic spots in the small garden. It was a small area that had hibiscus flowers that were blooming profusely in many different colors. It was a short distance from the fountain and the steps of the president's building. Students usually came there to take pictures.

There was nobody there now though, and it was quiet except for the breeze that was rustling the shrubs and the lone willow tree. It was the perfect spot to be right now. She was surprised when Clay followed her and even more surprised when he sat down across from her on the stone bench.

She pulled out her iPod and then paused. Clay looked like he wanted to talk but she was so not in the mood, even though it was refreshing to talk about Khaled with someone who did not immediately jump to conclusions about her mental state or accuse her of being obsessed. Besides, Clay was cute, in an understated kind of way. He had the kind of face that her writer friend, Sabrina, would say is perfect for the front of a novel.

He was slim without being too thin. A sculpted nose, level thick eyebrows, and almond shaped eyes with just a little crinkle at the sides indicating that he laughed a lot, or probably squinted into too many microscopes. He had medium brown, evenly colored skin, and straight white teeth.

She could see that he had worn braces as a kid, like her. That almost made her interested in him. She had vowed that she would only date someone who liked music or art, not someone who was overly 'sciencey' and analytical like Ramon.

This Clay guy was a science geek, even more so than Ramon. He had even finished his lab report before Ramon had finished his. Maybe he was only humoring her about Khaled in order to talk to her. It would not be the first time someone had used that strategy.

Jessica put down her earphones and decided to test him to see if he was a true fan.

"You say you like Khaled," she rubbed her chin, "what is his favorite color?"

"Red," Clay said. "He always has this red hibiscus design on his album covers. I heard that when he was younger his mother got sick, and before she died she planted a hibiscus bush in her garden just so that he could remember her."

Jessica nodded vigorously. "That's true. You really are a

fan"

Clay raised his eyebrow. "You were testing me?"

"Yes, because you are a science type, and I have no interest in science guys. They are too logical." Jessica straightened up dramatically and flashed her hand expressively, "I am more into the arts and music."

Clay struggled not to smile. "I can see that, but have you ever really thought that the Khaled story could be a hoax, a crazy story his people made up to sell more records, and make him look good?"

"Is that what you think?" Jessica said furiously. "One moment you are cool and the next moment you are not. If you want to talk to me, don't say anything bad about Khaled! You hear me? Never!"

"It wasn't something bad," Clay defended. "Okay, sorry." He held up his hand when Jessica actually growled at him. "Remember, I like his music too."

"You know, I write material for him. When all my friends were fantasizing about which local guy they wanted to be with, I would be picturing how I would meet Khaled and he'd instantly know that we were meant to be together, and then we'd do music together," Jessica mused. "I have a whole hardcover book of songs written just for Khaled."

"He's not dead, so technically he is not gone forever," Clay said. "Maybe one day he'll pop out of retirement. Artistes do it all the time."

Jessica shrugged. "I guess, but I am beginning to believe that it's growing up time for me. I have to put to rest my impossible fantasies about me and Khaled being together." She struggled so she wouldn't start crying. She didn't want Clay to think that she was a moron. "I am strange, I know," her voice choked up, "but I just feel so sad about this whole thing. I feel sad and empty and..."

"Lost," Clay finished for her. His deep brown eyes were gazing at her with empathy. "That usually happens when we give up our idols or when they die."

"He's not an idol to me," Jessica said faintly. "I know I am unusually attached to the singer but I don't worship him. I go to church, I read my Bible."

"And you have Khaled in very high esteem," Clay said, musing. "You have to admit he is good looking. You have pin-ups of him on your walls in your room, don't you?"

Jessica nodded reluctantly. "I do, but only because I like his voice."

Clay chuckled. "That makes sense."

"No, seriously," Jessica said. "If I didn't like his voice he wouldn't be a pin up. I mean I look at him and his songs come to mind."

"So can we hang out sometime?" Clay asked, changing the subject. He could see that if he wanted to get to know Jessica he would have to do some serious battling for her affections, and it was going to be a hard war. He had serious competition: Khaled, her obsession, and Ramon, her childhood friend with whom she had a great rapport. He was going to have to work hard to make it into Jessica's affections, but he was up for the challenge.

Jessica looked at him, "I don't think..."

"I can write poetry," Clay said quickly, "in fact I have a whole book of them. I am somewhat of a hybrid. I love the arts and the sciences, and I do a fairly decent poetic rendition."

"Really?" Jessica's golden eyes sparkled at him. "You are putting me on. What's your poem about: acid and alkaline kissing in a tube?"

Clay grinned. "You are funny. No, I write everyday-life sort of poems. I have been at Mount Faith for four months, since summer, trying to finish a degree that I started a long time ago. My family didn't like the decision, especially since I already had a job."

He smiled, "I have a lot of poems about loneliness, poems about following your dreams, and poems about God and his goodness."

"Oh," Jessica said. "Well then, the poetry society is having a poetry recital on The Greens this evening, at six. You can sit beside me. It is not a date."

Clay nodded. "Yes, ma'am."

Jessica got up. "I am going to my room to mourn in peace." Then she frowned and turned around. "So, if you are just coming back to finish a degree, how old are you?"

"Twenty-seven," Clay looked away and then back at her. "Is that too old?"

"No," Jessica said. "What were you doing before?"

She's interested in me. Clay's heart sung. Up until now she had been so preoccupied with Khaled that she had half-heartedly engaged him in conversation, but now he could see it in her eyes that she was registering that he was there.

"I worked with my uncle," Clay shrugged, "at a recording studio."

"You did?" Jessica's eyes widened. "Why didn't you say something? Did you know I am doing a degree in Music Composition and Technology?"

"You kinda alluded to that when you said you wanted to produce songs for Khaled," Clay said, shifting uncomfortably on the bench. He knew where this conversation was going and he didn't want to go there.

Jessica nodded. "Yes, that's right. Which studio were you working with?"

Clay paused so long that Jessica cleared her throat. "It's not a hard question you know, unless you were lying."

Clay sighed. "I was working with iJam."

"That's one of the biggest, most well known studios in Jamaica." She squealed, "That's Khaled's studio. Oh, my! Do you know Khaled?"

Clay nodded reluctantly. "Yes, I do."

"You do?" Jessica sat back down across from Clay and swallowed. "I have never met somebody who knows Khaled personally."

Clay was already regretting telling her. He could see her gearing up to ask him a million and one Khaled questions, and then it occurred to him that that would not necessarily be a bad thing. He could get to know her better in the process.

He thought about the first time he had seen her at the lab waiting at the glass door and peering at Ramon. Her short corkscrew curls had framed her piquant face. After a shaft of sunlight hit her hair, it had seemed that her curls turned to gold. He had dubbed her "the golden girl" in his thoughts.

He had started looking out for her after that, and wished that he could talk to her, but she was always hanging with Ramon, and now he was finding out that she was obsessed with Khaled. He wished that he hadn't opened his big mouth and told her that he knew Khaled. Now she would never want to find out anything about him. It would always be about Khaled.

He looked at Jessica, who still had her mouth opened. Her lips were naturally pink, and she was licking them in anticipation of asking him questions. He stared at them for a while and then said, "Well, here I am. Somebody who knows Khaled."

"What is he like in real life?" Jessica asked. "Is he a nice person? Is he nice to old people and kind to animals?"

Clay wondered if she wanted to hear the truth or the sanitized version meant for the public. He settled for an answer that wouldn't dim the stars he saw in her eyes for Khaled, but then he wondered if he was crazy.

"I guess he is okay. He really doesn't interact with the staff much but I have never seen him kick a dog."

"But," Jessica said, "he said in an interview once that he hangs out at the studio with the guys, and that you are all like a family."

Clay shrugged. "He's not really a talker. Maybe he said it so that he could look better, like he was a sociable kind of person, you know, or maybe his people crafted the script for him."

Jessica grimaced. "I get it. You don't like him much, do you?"

"Why'd you say that?" Clay frowned.

"Because every time I mention anything about Khaled you end up saying something snarky."

Jessica got up again. "See you later at the Greens. Don't be late either. I am keeping the seat beside me for no more than five minutes."

Clay grinned. "Okay. I'll keep that in mind."

Chapter Two

After his final class for the day, Clay drove into Blue Palm Apartments. His car's dashboard clock was five minutes fast; it read, five-thirty. He had just thirty-five minutes to shower, get dressed, search his poem book for a piece to impress Jessica, and show up at the Greens. The Greens was a lawn area behind the performing arts building that had an open theatre kind of feel.

He glanced at the clouds when he stepped out of his car and saw that it was overcast. *Please God, let it not rain,* he thought silently. The poetry recital would be a big distraction from her Khaled obsession and he wanted to make the most of the opportunity.

He almost bumped into a young woman who was dressed in a charcoal-colored suit. "Watch it," she hissed. She was carrying a square cake box. "This is my only way to get back with the in-crowd at the law fraternity. The whole snobby lot of them have shunned me, but they like cake."

"Sorry," he grinned.

She nodded stiffly then her eyes lit up when she looked at him fully. "Oh, it's you, my handsome neighbor from Apartment 1B."

"Yes," Clay nodded, "if you are in 1A then we are neighbors."

"Tracy Carr is the name," she said, holding out her hand cautiously while using her body to balance the box.

"Clay Reid." Clay watched the box carefully while he shook her hand.

"You know, we have a block party every September to welcome new tenants to Blue Palm. It is on Saturday night. You should come. We have a bonfire, eat s'mores, and meet and hangout with other people who live on the building."

"Well, I am not exactly new," Clay said, "I was around in the summer."

"Ah," Tracy nodded. "You are still new to us. What are you doing up here? Surely you aren't a freshman? You don't look fresh, and I say that in a good way."

"I am a chemistry major. I came back to finish a couple of courses. My uncle said that Mount Faith is a laid-back school so it is the perfect place for me to finish my degree. I have this thing where I have to finish what I started. I should be graduating next year."

"Well, good for you." Tracy smiled. "Listen, I am looking forward to seeing you at the bonfire. If you ever need anything, just holler at me next door. This is my final year as well. I am doing law."

"I got that," Clay nodded, "and you fell out with your frat members."

"Over something so petty only idiots would have me up for that." Tracy shook her head. "See you later."

"Later," Clay watched as she carefully placed the cake in

the back of her car and then drove off.

He looked at his watch. Yikes, he only had twenty minutes to meet Jessica and he did not want her to give his seat to someone else.

*****

When he arrived at The Greens he realized that it was well attended, mainly by artsy students. He stopped counting how many persons were attending when he got to fifty.

Weak sunrays made their way through the overcast skies and lit up the lawn to a golden glint. Jessica waved to him from the second row and he went over to sit with her. She looked gorgeous in the fading sunlight. She had on a yellow blouse and a yellow headband that kept her wild curls from her face. Her beautiful caramel skin looked like it was glowing in the waning sun.

"Hey," she said when he sat beside her. "I kept your seat."

"Thanks." Clay smiled at her, unable to look away. She smelled good and looked good. She was like a breath of fresh air. He wanted to savor this image of her, but high-energy Jessica wouldn't sit still, and she quickly turned to somebody beside her and was talking animatedly.

"Oops, sorry," she said, turning to Clay, "this is my friend, Davia. She is dating my cousin, Vanley. She is practically family too, soon to be Mrs. Bancroft."

She leaned back so that he could see the girl, who was looking quite pleased at the introduction.

Davia smiled at him. "Hey."

"Hey," was all he could muster before someone took the microphone that was in the middle of the makeshift stage and cleared her throat. The microphone made a squealing sound that had everybody cupping their ears. When the microphone noise stopped, the girl on stage, who looked to be in her late teens, and who was attired in a white 'floaty' dress, clutched the microphone and said solemnly, "Hi everyone. My name is Emily. I am kicking off the poetry readings this evening with my poem 'Hush'."

The mumblings died down as everyone focused on Emily.

"Hush," Emily said, vigorously contorting her face into a caricature of pain.

"Hush," she said again, more vigorously this time.

"Hush," she squealed in the night air.

"Hush!" She belted it out so loudly that the microphone squealed again.

She said "hush" twenty more times, each time pausing between her squealing, then she walked off the stage. Her face was wet with sweat, and she was trembling from the energy it must have taken her to put on the performance.

People were cheering and clapping their fingers in appreciation, but Clay was trying hard to hold in a laugh that was on the verge of bursting out. He looked at Jessica, who looked like she was having the same challenge.

"Hush," Jessica said to him. "If you make me laugh..."

Clay chuckled, and then he burst out laughing. Then he realized that Jessica had joined him, leaning on him, her slim frame shaking. He liked that. He almost stopped laughing to better appreciate her womanly curves resting on his side.

Davia was chuckling. "You two stop it. The girl did her squealing best."

That, of course, sent them over the edge, with Davia joining in.

The subsequent poems were not so bad. Some were profound, and others were just okay. Jessica went up for the freestyle section. "Hey, everyone," Jessica said softly. "This poem was written today when a particular dream of mine died. I wrote it in my sadness, so excuse me if it sounds a bit morbid:

You may not understand it, but he was my dream.
His voice like tentacles surrounded me,
Trapped me in his world.
His words like honey ensnared me,
And after a while I didn't want to be free.

In my mind, he was mine
And I was his,
What a dream, how foolish..."

Her poem had four stanzas, each one as hopeless as the previous. Clay looked at Jessica when she returned to her seat. "You feel that strongly about Khaled?"

"Yup," Jessica said, "but I am sure it will get better some day. Whatever this is that I have for him will eventually die."

Clay resisted taking her hand in his and squeezing it with reassurance. He looked out on the lawn instead. The paper lanterns that they had strewn over the theatre area were rocking to a gentle wind. He drew his jacket closer to himself.

"It was a good poem," he whispered, "I would cut each verse to three lines and use the part where you said, 'in my mind, he was mine, and I was his, what a dream, how foolish,' as a chorus. I actually like it."

"For real?" Jessica looked at him interestedly. "You think Khaled would sing it?"

"Most definitely," Clay said. "Your emotions sound very much like those he expresses in his latest album. It was unhappy, wasn't it?"

"Are you criticizing him again?" Jessica hissed. "Because if you are..."

"No," Clay said, "it's just that his last album sounded like he was fed up. I could hear anger and a bit of depression in it; it was quite unlike his first five albums. He must have been feeling some sort of uneasiness to sing those songs with such emotions."

"Yes," Jessica frowned. "You are right. You are really good at this analysis thing aren't you?"

Clay grinned. "I told you: I'm an hybrid."

"A man who loves music, a man who loves art." Jessica whispered.

"Respects the spirit world and thinks with his heart." Clay whispered back. "That's me. Are you ready for love, Jessica?"

They were whispering so loudly that the persons behind them started mumbling for them to shut up.

Jessica was looking at him transfixed after he asked her that question. She knew that they were quoting from India Arie's song, but he had asked her seriously, and something inside her had silently responded.

"Want to go get a drink at the Business Center?" Clay asked.

"Sure," Jessica said, snapping out of her contemplation. She turned to Davia to tell her goodbye and then she turned back to him.

They walked around the Performance Arts Building to the side where they had the outdoor sculptures. Jessica was moving so swiftly that Clay found that he was practically panting to keep up with her. "Wait, Jess. I was thinking of a slow walk, you know, like a stroll?"

Jessica smirked. "Sorry, I was thinking." She was actually thinking about him and how her heart leaped when he asked if she was ready for love: real love, with a real guy. She took slower steps. "How am I doing?"

"Much better," Clay said, slowing his pace to fit hers. "Do

you always have this much energy?"

"Only at nights. I am nocturnal." Jessica smiled. "When dark covers the land I am infused with a burst of energy, but I tend to wilt in the mornings."

Clay laughed. "I guess I am nocturnal as well. I am more creative at nights."

"I forgot that we have that music thing in common." Jessica turned to him, "What did you do at your uncle's studio?"

"Everything," Clay said. "I was a jack of all trades. I could practically run the place by myself…technical stuff… production, that sort of thing. I also write songs for artistes."

"So, why are you studying science?" Jessica looked at him in the half-light.

"I finish what I start." Clay shrugged. "I also wanted a break from the studio, so I thought why not take this year and finish my degree. I only had a year of courses left to do anyway."

They entered the courtyard at the Business Center. Students were still milling around there.

"Let's get ice cream," Jessica said, "instead of a drink."

Clay shuddered. To him the night was very chilly, but obviously it was no problem to Jessica. "Sure, why not?" he said valiantly, hoping that his teeth didn't chatter when he sat down to eat with her.

Clay got a small cup of frozen yogurt and was eating it slowly. They were now sitting near the fountain, in front of a potted palm.

"So tell me about you, Jessica. I really don't know anything about you except your love for Khaled."

He silently chastised himself for bringing up Khaled's name. He didn't want Jessica to be sad again or start discussing him. It didn't seem to affect her because she said lightly, "I love vanilla ice cream." She innocently licked the ice cream that was running down the side of the cone; looking at him, not realizing that her little pink tongue was creating havoc in his body.

Clay looked at her, mesmerized, then looked away. She was eating her ice cream innocently, and had no intent to seduce him, but there he was, thinking dirty thoughts.

"I would have tagged you as some exotic flavor," Clay said, "like sour sop or guava."

"This is going to sound really fanatic, and it probably is," Jessica said, "but one day I read that Khaled likes vanilla, and since then I have felt that vanilla tastes right somehow."

"Jessica, I work with celebrities. I am sorry to say, but most of what those celebrities tell you is rubbish. You know that, right?"

Jessica paused her eating. "Does Khaled like vanilla ice cream?"

"No, he doesn't," Clay said. "Maybe in the interview he said he liked vanilla because that was a neutral flavor, something that most people can identify with. You know Jessica, when you have a publicist most of what is said in the public domain is carefully thought out. Many things are targeted to the core fans so that they can identify with the brand."

"Jessica mused. You worked in the business; you must be right. I am a stone cold idiot. Aren't I?"

"No," Clay said, "just a tad naïve." He put down his yogurt. The thing was making him chillier than he was already feeling. He looked at Jessica and grinned, "I think you are way too involved with Khaled."

"I know, I know." Jessica laughed. "My Mom has been on my case since recently to burn my Khaled tapes and start acting my age. She has this bee in her bonnet that when she was twenty-one she was already married and pregnant with my brother, Micah, and was running her own house. She says it so often these days that I think she is hinting that I should move out of the house. What do you think?"

Clay shrugged. "I don't know your mother, but I know that parents like it when their children settle in a happy relationship with someone they like and know well. I understand why you having a fantasy over a guy like Khaled would worry her, especially at your age."

"What's your Mom like?" Jessica finished her ice cream and wiped her lips. "Does she hound you to settle down and find yourself a wife?" She looked at the crinkle lines at the side of his eyes as he laughed at the question.

He went from cute to really handsome when he laughed. She laughed with him. Even though she didn't intend her question to be funny, it felt good to be talking to a human being who actively listened to her, especially since not many persons in her life really listened to her. It made for a nice change, and even though Clay had recently walked into her life, she realized that she had good chemistry with him.

"My mother doesn't hound me," Clay said. "She is concerned about my relationships, yes, but I think she is even more concerned about my relationship with God and stuff. She hates the studio; she hardly comes by because she thinks that everybody there drinks and does drugs."

"Do they?" Jessica asked breathlessly.

Clay chuckled. "Oh, no, not at iJam. We are a very professional outfit. If that sort of thing were going on there, my Mom wouldn't allow me to work there in the first place. I used to go there in the evenings after high school to spend time with my uncle. That's where I learned everything I know now about the business."

"What about your Dad? Where's he?" Jessica asked.

"My Dad works on a ship. He is only home three months

out of the year. Since I was little it has always been Mommy and me. My uncle Neil has been there for me as well "

"Mommy's boy," Jessica said teasingly.

"Daddy's girl," Clay teased back.

"Not really," Jessica said. "All my siblings think that I am Daddy's favorite, but it is only because I am the youngest and I still live at home, and I make no waves in the family. All my siblings are colorful, but I am like that vanilla ice cream I just ate."

"Surely, that can't be true," Clay said, looking at her expressive face. "You seem like you are the life of every party, the center of attention for your family."

"Nah," Jessica said. "That center-of-attention honor definitely goes to my oldest brother, Micah. He is a loner and remarkably laid back, but for some reason he raises Daddy's blood pressure sky high on a regular basis. A few months ago he secretly married his fiancée, Charlene, at the courthouse without telling anyone."

Clay chuckled. "How did your parents take it?"

"Like always." Jessica grinned, "There was a family meeting. Daddy screamed, and Mommy cried, while Micah sat in a corner and ignored us. To make things worse with Dad, Micah quit his job at the university so he can focus on his farming. He has several greenhouses, which he is now running with his wife."

"He used to work here?" Clay said, enjoying watching her as she spoke about her family.

"Yes. He ran the whole operation at the Business Center." She looked around. "It always feels a little odd coming by without going up to Micah's office."

"So you have one older brother to chase the boys away?"

"One, goodness no!" Jessica grinned. "I have three brothers besides Micah. We are a pretty large clan. There is Taj. He's really the eldest of us; he has a different surname, but that's another story. He heads the Psychiatry Center. Then there is Adrian. He and his wife, Cathy, have two children. They visit the house quite often, so I see them all the time. And then there is Marcus. He is currently the most interesting and famous of us all. He won a gold medal at last year's Olympics. I also have a sister, Kylie, who is pregnant, but she is not a happy pregnant lady. Apparently her belly is hampering her from crouching over the computer." Jessica laughed. "I actually saw her trying to do it. It's funny, but really, I am happy for her and her husband, Gareth, even though they are already planning to have me baby-sit, not that I mind."

Clay chuckled. "You know, I had no idea that Marcus Bancroft was your brother."

Jessica looked at him incredulously. "Really?"

Clay shrugged. "Sorry. I am not as current as I should be. I heard his story though. A few months after losing his memory and breaking his legs, he won the 400 meters. That story was really inspirational. I watched it in the studio with the rest of the crew. I could swear some of the guys were crying."

"They were?" Jessica asked brightly. "Was Khaled there?"

Clay groaned inwardly. Why on earth couldn't he remember to stop mentioning the studio?

"He was there," Clay said reluctantly.

"So he knows about my brother" Jessica remarked craftily. "That means he is just one step away from knowing me."

Clay quickly changed back the subject to Jessica's family. "So did you go to the games last year?"

"Yes," Jessica said. "It was like a family reunion, and it was even sweeter because Marcus won his pet event and came second in his other one."

Clay smiled. "I can say that I truly envy you for your family. You guys seem so normal and close knit."

"You are an only child, huh?" Jessica giggled, "I can't imagine how that feels. My siblings are so involved in my life; it doesn't matter that they have their own families and should be minding their own businesses. They just like rifling into mine."

Clay was going to clarify what he meant about his family, but Jessica, in her high-energy style, had moved on, and he almost breathed a sigh of relief that she had. What was he doing? He had only met her today and already he was about to spew family secrets.

Jessica was about to ask Clay about his poetry book, but she glanced at the entrance to the Business Center and saw Ramon. She almost waved at him, but then she saw Helen Hines frantically waving and blowing kisses at him from the other side of the room. She stiffened.

"I can't believe he's seeing Helen Hines," Jessica said, feeling shell-shocked.

"Who?" Clay looked confused. Jessica's emotions could be so mercurial. One minute they were talking about her family and she was laughing with him, and the next she was scowling, a fierce frown on her slightly flushed face.

"Ramon 'Stupid' Rodriguez," Jessica said huffily. "That science prig, scum of the earth, old betrayer."

"I thought you two weren't together." Clay looked confused.

"We're not, but he is supposed to tell me if he's seeing anyone. It's a deal we made." Jessica sighed and aggressively wiped her mouth with the napkin that she had gotten with the ice cream, leaving some of the paper on her face.

Clay was about to point it out to her, but he didn't get the chance.

"I am going home. Today sucked big time. First Khaled, now Ramon."

She got up and left a puzzled Clay staring at her retreating back.

Chapter Three

"**D**o you think I have feelings for Ramon?" Jessica asked her cousin, Arnella. She was sitting in a colorful corner of Arnella's studio.

Arnella was painting birds and had various easels strewn around the studio with paintings of birds in mid-flight, birds bathing in water, and birds in pose. It was beautiful. A wealthy bird lover had commissioned several bright-colored pieces to match his decor.

Jessica figured that Arnella was only half-listening to her because she had been agreeing with every thing she had asked her so far. Her suspicions were confirmed when Arnella mumbled 'yes' to her Ramon question as she painted a bright orange swipe across her blank canvas then looked at it as if she had just done something marvelous. It was a simple stroke, one orange line across a blank canvas, so Jessica concluded that Arnella was looking through her mind's eye and was not really focusing on her present environment nor

Jessica's relationship issues.

Jessica grinned impishly and decided to test if Arnella was even listening by teasing her about her boyfriend, Alric. "Alric sent me a note yesterday saying he liked me."

Arnella was still staring at her canvas, and in the same monotone with which she had answered the other questions, said, "No, he didn't."

"So you really are listening?" Jessica asked cautiously.

"Yes," Arnella replied slowly. After several moments, she finally broke eye contact with her canvas and looked at Jessica fully.

"So far you've said that last Thursday you found out that Khaled retired. Same day you found out that Ramon was seeing Helen Fugly Hines. Is that really her name, 'Fugly'? And then you asked me if you have feelings for Ramon, to which I answered 'yes'."

"So you were listening, and no her name isn't 'Fugly'. She's actually pretty but I am not exactly objective now, am I?" Jessica sighed. "So why do you think I have feelings for Ramon?"

Arnella shrugged, "I don't know, it could have something to do with the fact that you guys have been so tight for years. I got the feeling that Ramon was waiting for you to grow out of your Khaled stage and was biding his time to be with you. Fine time too. You are too old for all that Khaled nonsense."

Jessica frowned, "I did not have a Khaled stage."

Arnella pointed her brush at Jessica. "That's what everybody knows you for Jessica Bancroft: Khaled this, Khaled that. There was no room for Ramon. My two cents is that this Khaled guy needed to retire or die for you to wake up from your slumber. His retirement is a good thing. It means no new music for you to look forward to and no imagining that he is singing to you, which is ridiculous by the way. Go and talk to Ramon. He's your best friend; tell him you have feelings for him."

"But I don't," Jessica said. "I like Ramon, I really do, but I don't think we have that connection, you know—no shivers down my spine. I just can't picture being with Ramon."

"Because you have been picturing being with Khaled. You just need to reset. Maybe you have suppressed it?" Arnella asked. "Didn't you feel jealous when you saw him with Heather?"

"Helen," Jessica corrected. "Yes, I sorta did. I even got up and left that guy I was talking to, Clay."

"Mmm," Arnella folded her arms. She was in a white paint-splattered t-shirt, and she added a smudge of orange to it. "So you were on a date with someone as well?"

"Sort of." Jessica shrugged. "Clay likes poetry and he likes Khaled too, so I invited him to our poetry concert."

Arnella nodded imitating Taj Jackson, her former psychiatrist, "So tell me about this Clay."

"He is good-looking, especially when he smiles. He has this way about him, but I can't pinpoint exactly what it is." Jessica mused. "He has an attractive maturity. You know, not stiff and overbearing. I don't know; I just like him."

Arnella frowned. "So what about Ramon?"

"I have known Ramon since I was three," Jessica said. "We went to the same prep school, the same high school, we celebrate the same birthday, and hang out together. He feels like my brother most of the time, when he's not being super-annoying."

Arnella raised her eyebrow. "Really? Brotherly love?"

"Yes." Jessica started massaging her scalp hoping for some revelation to pop up in her head regarding her mixed-up, topsy-turvy feelings toward Ramon. "But then there was that feeling of possessiveness last night. I can't believe I was jealous. It's like incest. I feel so dirty and weird."

"I don't think Ramon has the same kind of brotherly feelings toward you as you do toward him," Arnella said. "Have you looked in the mirror lately? You are pretty, and you are fun to be around, and so energetic and full of life. Ramon probably does not want to upset the relationship he has with you so he is moving on with Hillary."

"Helen," Jessica murmured once more. She was beginning to think that Arnella was deliberately mispronouncing Helen's name wrong.

"The guy is twenty-one, not twelve. He has man feelings for you, while you go crazy over a singer. Boy, I feel it for Ramon." Arnella shook her head.

Jessica looked at Arnella throughout the whole assessment of her situation, knowing with certainty that Arnella was right, but at the same time irritated by her cousin for her plain speaking. She now wished that Arnella would just go back to her canvas and stop dispensing painful hard assessments, especially the one where she practically called her a case of arrested development.

She was itching to get up and storm out of Arnella's studio, but that would be immature. She inhaled. "That was harsh."

Arnella smiled. "You came to me for the truth. You could have gone to your sister, or your brothers, but you wanted someone to shake you out of your stupor. You are most welcome, now go and sort out your life."

Arnella turned back to her painting.

"I hate it when you think you are right, and I hate the way you spout out those stinging words," Jessica said getting up.

Arnella picked up her paintbrush and chuckled. "I hate it that you are bright and pretty and have your whole life spread out before you to enjoy but yet you live an active fantasy life with a guy you have never met and who doesn't know you exist. Wake up, look around, do something about Ramon, or that Clay guy, before they disappear."

*****

Jessica waited for Ramon's Chemistry Dynamics class to end. She was sitting in the lounge area of the science building. She was facing the glass doors that lead to the entrance of the lecture theatre; as soon as he came out, she would know. She had thirty minutes to wait. She took out her iPod and then dropped it back in her bag. She was about to let Khaled keep her company, but since Arnella's speech yesterday she was rethinking her every action as it regarded Khaled.

She glanced at her watch; thirty minutes seemed to be crawling unnecessarily slowly. She twiddled her thumbs and shifted in the chair. She wished that she had carried a book to read. There was a stack of Chemistry Today magazines on the center table in the lounge. They still looked glossy and untouched.

She considered picking up one but thought better of it. If not even chemistry students were reading it, why should she? If this were the Creative and Performing Arts Center, the arts magazines would be dog-eared from having been well-thumbed through, if there were even any left on the table.

She glanced at her watch again and realized that barely a minute had ticked by. She reluctantly reached for the magazine. The headline article was *The Role of Selenium in Chemical Biology.*

"Oh, joy," she said out loud.

Clay chuckled behind her. "It's actually interesting."

Jessica swiveled around to look at him, almost cracking her neck in the process.

"Clay! I owe you an apology." She gripped the magazine close to her chest. "I know I walked away from you last Thursday without saying a proper goodbye, but I was a bit traumatized."

Clay nodded. "I could see that." He walked around the sofa and sat beside her. "So how are you doing?"

"Fine," Jessica paused, "getting by without Khaled, trying to act my age. I am having withdrawal symptoms." She pointed to her iPod. "Serious withdrawal symptoms."

Clay regarded her, an indefinable expression in his eyes. He didn't respond to what she said, and Jessica looked him over, suddenly feeling uncomfortable.

He was dressed in blue jeans and a blue checkered shirt. He looked very attractive, more so than he did last week Thursday. Jessica shook her head inwardly. She had to get a grip. She couldn't think of Clay this way. After all, she was sitting in the lobby waiting for Ramon to put Arnella's theory to the test. She wanted to see if he was attracted to her and was waiting for her to quit Khaled.

Well, she hadn't quite gotten Khaled out of her head, and she was not going to quit cold turkey, but here was Clay, looking as handsome as ever, creating a tension in her that she didn't quite know how to handle.

"You have orange paint in your hair," he finally said.

"I know," Jessica said jerkily. She was feeling shy and nervy. The emotion was so new to her that she almost gasped. What was happening to her?

"I went to visit my cousin's studio yesterday, and she was waving her brush around, lecturing me about..."

"About?" Clay asked when she slumped back in the chair and squeezed her eyes shut.

"How immature I am," Jessica mumbled, "the usual lecture about Khaled that everybody takes pleasure in imparting when I am around."

Clay smiled, and Jessica watched as his mouth curled slowly. She felt that little nervousness return to her body. She was twitching because of it and couldn't make eye contact with him just then.

"What's wrong?" Clay asked as she lowered her eyes.

"I don't know." Jessica moaned. "I think my nervous system is short circuiting or something."

Clay bent down his head and looked at her. "The first time I saw you I think my nervous system short circuited too. It was a Wednesday afternoon, the first day of summer school. You leaned against the door and looked around. Your eyes met mine briefly, too briefly for you to register, but it meant a lot to me, and I think I had some circuitry problems then."

His eyes were serious as he said this, and Jessica bit her lip from trembling. He even looked good from upside down. Jessica closed her eyes and swallowed.

"I can't deal with this feeling right now. I am supposed to be talking to Ramon about our relationship."

Clay straightened up. "You two are going to take your relationship to a romantic level?"

"Well, apparently I am suppressing my feelings for him, and now that I have decided to give up my Khaled fantasy, it is probably time for us to move on to another level."

Clay sighed. "That seems so clinical. If it's time you should know it in here."

He touched her on her green t-shirt, right in the center, near her racing heart. Jessica felt her heart hammering long after he withdrew his hand. She licked her lips and looked out toward the glass door. The first wave of students was now coming through the door.

She looked at the big clock on the wall. She was agitated, and she knew that Clay could see her discomfort. She just wanted him, and his unsettling presence, to move away so that she could properly assess what was happening to her.

She looked at him from the sides of her eyes. He was looking at the doors as well.

"I was invited to a bonfire at my apartment building on Saturday night. Want to come? Just as friends." He said this hurriedly, while still not looking at her.

Jessica cleared her throat. "What time... er... does it start?"

"Don't know," Clay said, "Come at eight. You can hang out with me till they are ready. No pressure."

But I am pressured, Jessica thought. Quite out of the blue, she was horrendously attracted to Clay Reid.

Clay got up. "I would wish you well with Ramon, but that would be a conflict of interest. See you on Saturday." He waved to her and walked toward the doors, almost brushing against Ramon, who was on his way out.

Ramon had headed straight to the cafeteria after class. Jessica walked beside him, filling up his brooding silence with inane chatter. He collected his food at the station, and they sat at the back of the cafeteria in their usual spot.

"Why are you so quiet?" Jessica asked.

"Nobody can get in a word when you start," Ramon said, chewing on his second burger. His hair was overly long, and some of it was flopping onto his forehead. Jessica assessed him while she drummed her fingers on the table. She wasn't hungry so she had not taken a lunch. She was free to ogle Ramon as much as she wanted. His face was as familiar to her as her own. She looked at him: his wavy black hair, his olive complexion, and his oval face.

Both his parents were doctors at the Mount Faith Teaching Hospital. His father was head of cardiology, and his mother was a general practitioner who some referred to as Doctor "Panadol" Rodriguez because she prescribed it so frequently.

They had come from Columbia to Jamaica to stay for a few years, only going back for holidays. They had two children, Ramon and Henri; both boys had followed in their scientific footsteps.

Henri was doing his residency at the Medical Center at Mount Faith and Ramon was doing Chemistry. The next step for Ramon would be medical school, then internship at the hospital, then marriage, then boring little Rodriguez babies who would want to walk in their dad's footsteps.

Jessica almost snored at the picture in her mind. No music, no art, no energy. Ramon especially hated music, or did he just hate Khaled? She didn't know. During the many years that they grew up together, she couldn't pinpoint anything remotely artsy that Ramon was ever interested in.

She drummed her finger on the table again, struggling to come up with any common ground that she and Ramon shared. They liked to watch animal documentaries together; they liked the same foods, and they were born on June 1 of the same year. He was a tad bit shorter than her though. She was beginning to realize, after looking at her best friend for several moments, that she was always the one to dictate what activities they did together.

She had always been the dominant in her relationship with Ramon. Sometimes he protested, other times he just gave in. Did he really like her in a romantic kind of way? She doubted that the more she thought about it; but she decided to test Arnella's theory.

She touched his hand to see if her heart raced as it did when Clay had touched her. There was nothing. Maybe she was doing it the wrong way. She gently brushed his hair-covered arm with hers—still nothing.

"What are you doing?" Ramon asked in mid-chew, staring at her as if she were an alien.

"Checking for chemistry, a rush of blood to the head, a tingling in the spine, that sort of thing," Jessica said, brushing his hand again.

Ramon was still looking at her like she had two heads. "Why are you checking if you and me have chemistry?"

"Because since I have been trying to give up Khaled, I realize that I should stop living in a fantasy world and start living in the here and now. Since you must have a thing for me through all these years because I am pretty and full of life, I am giving a romantic relationship with you a try."

Ramon started coughing, and Jessica quickly realized that he was really laughing. He swallowed the burger prematurely and started choking. After a thump in the back from Jessica, he was fine. He laughed so hard he fell out of his chair and kept laughing on the ground. Tears were running down his cheeks by the time he recovered enough to say, "I love you, Jess."

"You do?" Jessica asked, dismay written all over her face. "What kind of love?"

Ramon panted. "I love you like I always have. You make me laugh. You have so much energy. You are like my sister, for heavens sake."

"That's what I told Arnella," Jessica said, relief coursing through her body. "She had this idea that you were waiting for me to get over Khaled before dating me."

"I did," Ramon said, "four years ago when I took you to senior dance. I was mad jealous of Khaled too. You spoke about him for 90% of the time. I was going to ask you to be my girlfriend then."

"I didn't realize..."

"I know." Ramon shrugged. "I thought Khaled was just too much competition. I sobered up soon after that dance and realized that you were too much for me to handle anyhow."

"I am?" Jessica asked. "What does that mean?"

"I am quiet. You are high voltage," Ramon said. "We are super incompatible and I know it. When I accepted that, things went back to normal in my mind, though it did take a long while."

Jessica grimaced. "High voltage. I sound like electricity."

"It feels that way sometimes," Ramon said. "After a livewire session with you, I have to recharge my batteries to handle exposure to you the following day."

"I sound toxic too." Jessica grinned, understanding exactly what he was saying. She pinched him, twisting his skin savagely.

"Ouch," Ramon howled. "What was that for?"

"I saw you with Helen last Thursday."

"She likes me." Ramon grinned wickedly. "She is wonderfully un-melodramatic and quiet, with the right amount of energy for me," Ramon said, sipping his drink, and grimacing. "Whoever made this drink must have stayed at a distance and thrown in the sugar, granule by granule."

Jessica chuckled in relief. They were back to normal. "Why didn't you tell me about Helen. We promised each other that we would say whenever we have another person in our lives."

"You mean like you told me about Clay?" Ramon asked. "I saw you two on Thursday night too."

"But that was a spur of the moment thing. I invited him to a poetry concert. It wasn't a date."

Ramon wriggled his brow. "Madam Jessica, I think we have what you would call an impasse. Meeting Helen was a spur of the moment thing too. I went to the Business Center to eat and she was there."

"Okay, okay." Jessica sat up straighter. "I like Clay"

"What? Am I hearing right?" Ramon asked jokingly.

"Jessica likes a guy who is not Khaled." He mused, finally putting down the cup. "Why doesn't Khaled have a last name?"

"I don't know," Jessica shrugged. "He's just Khaled, like Cher is just Cher, and Sade is just Sade."

"So what's his real name then?" Ramon asked. "You must know that. He's been your phantom crush for years."

"I don't know. There is no info on that."

"On the Internet?" Ramon shook his head. "Something's not right. No mother gets up and says, 'this is my child, his name is just Khaled.'"

" For you, nothing is ever right about Khaled," Jessica said.

"One day when I have loads of time on my hands, I am going to find out what Khaled's full name is," Ramon promised. "So have you kissed Clay yet? Remember how you used to fantasize that your first kiss would be with Khaled under an umbrella in the rain with the elements crashing around you?"

"Shut up." Jessica frowned. "I have a way to go, but I am growing up. It sucks that I told you so many things."

"Fantasies, all featuring Khaled." Ramon laughed. "Anyway, I am happy you are growing up. Welcome to the land of the living. Maybe we should carry our significant others with us for lunch and have a double date."

"Maybe," Jessica said noncommittally, though it gave her a warm feeling to think of Clay as her significant other.

Chapter Four

Clay walked into the lab sleepily. He had stayed up the night before torturing himself with the thought of Jessica and Ramon finally moving their friendship to a romantic level.

He had found the girl that he didn't even know he was searching for, and she chose just that moment to explore a romantic relationship with her longtime friend. The thought was depressing and gave him a heavy feeling. He sat down beside his lab partner, Stewart, who had his head on the desk.

"What's up mate, didn't sleep well either?" he asked Stewart.

Stewart looked up at him, his eyes bloodshot, and said hoarsely, "Ray Cummings is sleeping with my girlfriend."

Clay frowned. "Ray Cummings?"

"Yes, the nerd, our lab instructor." Stewart sighed. "If he can get my girlfriend to sleep with him. I don't know man..."

"How do you know she's sleeping with him?" Clay asked while he took out his lab book.

"Because twice I saw him sneaking out of her place at Blue Palm Apartments."

Stewart put his head back on his arms. "I am going to kill him."

"No," Clay said hurriedly. "No girl is worth going to jail for."

"She's worth it." Stewart heaved a sigh. "I can't tell you how much she's worth it. Tracy is the best thing to ever happen to me. No man is going to come between us."

"Then you should take that up with Tracy, not Ray. Sort it out with her." Then something clicked with Clay, Tracy from Blue Palm Apartments was probably his neighbor. "Is your girlfriend's full name Tracy Carr?"

"Yeah, man." Stewart straightened up. "You know her?"

"Met her last week…very friendly. She's a law student?"

"That's her." Stewart nodded. "And the best debater ever. She knows her stuff."

Clay nodded. "Maybe you should talk to her about Ray."

"She's going to deny it." Stewart frowned. "Tracy and I have been together for the whole summer. I know how she argues, and I know that she'll have some excuse for having Ray in her apartment at two o'clock in the morning. Just yesterday he was there until four o'clock."

Clay realized that Stewart was beyond reasoning. He was seething with hatred. He felt like warning Ray to watch out when he stepped into the classroom, his white lab coat almost engulfing his small frame.

He was a short and extremely slim guy who had a wide mouth. He was self-conscious about his prominent overbite so he rarely smiled, and he had oily skin that broke out periodically. Clay had had him as a lab instructor in the summer and he was still in awe at how well Ray knew his science. He was like a genius squared. This was also Ray's final year as a chemistry student. Ray was going to make waves in the science world; he was sure of that.

He looked at the bristling Stewart who had straightened up when the door opened and Ray walked through.

Stewart was undeniably handsome and he dressed very well. He took pride in flexing his biceps so that women could stare at him. Clay almost laughed at the irony of Stewart being jealous over Ray. Maybe Tracy Carr was really more interested in brains than brawn. If she was, she would be a real anomaly in the female world, based on his experience.

He almost grinned at Stewart's intense scowl then his eyes zeroed in on Ramon, reminding him that he had some girl trouble as well.

He was still feeling the effects of tossing and turning and thinking about Jessica. She had all but admitted that she was attracted to him just before she went off with Ramon to pursue their relationship. Every word had been like a dagger to his heart.

"Today we are going to learn how to make gun powder," Ray said, interrupting his thoughts. "It's a pretty simple combination of potassium nitrate, charcoal, and elemental sulphur. Did you know that in the past people would obtain potassium nitrate from bat guano or horse urine?"

"He is the horse urine." Stewart mumbled darkly.

Clay listened as Ray explained the various elements and the process they would use to make gunpowder. He was jotting down notes even though he could barely hear Ray. Every time he spoke, Stewart grumbled something derogatory about him.

"Here's the kicker, though," Ray said. "I want you to find out what quantity of each ingredient is required and then next week we will make the explosive. The finer the powder, the faster it will burn, so come prepared to work. We will need an extra hour for lab, so work it out with your other classes."

Ray gave them one of his rare smiles, his yellow uneven teeth gleaming. Stewart shuddered beside him. "I can't believe that she kissed him. Somebody pinch me. Wake me up."

Clay growled. "Snap out of it, Stewart."

He wished that they didn't have to have the same lab partner all semester because Stewart was going to be a pain. He couldn't even remember how he was saddled with him in the first place.

After class, Clay watched Ramon. He was asking Ray questions about the gunpowder experiment, and Ray was patiently answering him. Clay was itching to ask him about Jessica. Were they now officially together?

He had no right to be feeling this way about her. He came on the scene just three months ago; Ramon and Jessica were friends for years. He should stop thinking about her as much as he was. He was just setting up himself for heartbreak. Jessica and Ramon had history. He sighed.

"Sounds like I am not the only one with issues," Stewart said beside him. "What do you have to sigh about?"

Clay shrugged, "I like a girl; she has a boyfriend."

Stewart scowled, "Jessica Bancroft. I see the way you've been staring at her all summer. Leave the girl alone then. Don't intrude on her relationship with her guy."

"I will." Clay stuffed his notes into his bag. "I hope your situation works out."

"It will," Stewart scowled, "because I have a plan."

Clay looked at him warningly. "Don't do it... whatever it is."

Stewart looked as if he wasn't listening to him. He had zoned out. Clay walked away, nodding at Ramon's enthusiastic wave as he went through the door. He could see that Ramon was happy. He almost scowled at him and headed through the door in a huff.

*****

"What put you in such a bad mood?" Jessica was sitting on the bottom step below the lab door. She had been reading a book, and now it was lying face down on her lap as she contemplated him through slit eyes.

He couldn't prevent the grin that slipped across his face. She was lovely to behold. She had on a pink top and black jeans. Her usually wild hair was in a ponytail.

He sat beside her. "I had a rough night. I was thinking about you and Ramon…The truth is, he just waved to me and I got angry, jealous really."

Jessica gasped. "You really like me that much?"

"Yeah." Clay nodded. "I thought I told you before."

"Well," Jessica grinned, "I can't remember. Tell me again."

"I like you; I haven't liked a girl this much since…ever." Clay looked at her seriously. "And you are now with Ramon; that sucks."

"I am not with Ramon." Jessica touched her hand to his and then drew it away, gasping. They definitely had the chemistry she was searching for.

"I thought you were planning to get together with him." Clay asked, confused.

"Well, we didn't," Jessica said breezily. "We are back to normal, Ramon and I. I was waiting for you just now."

"You were?" Clay grinned, feeling a relief so deep, it was making him dizzy.

"Yes." Jessica stood up and brushed off her pants. "The poetry society is having a reading in the cafeteria. It starts in five minutes. I thought we could have lunch while listening to poems. I did a poem, want to hear it?"

Clay nodded eagerly. He would love to hear anything from her, even if it were rubbish.

"It's called Letting Go." Jessica cleared her throat. "It is hard to move from the familiar, give yourself breathing room, it will always seem as if it is too soon, but in order to grow, you should know that you have to let it go..."

When she finished speaking, Clay was silent.

"So, do you like it?"

"It was perfect," Clay said softly. "I really liked it. What familiar thing are you letting go?"

Jessica swallowed. It was Khaled, but she didn't want to say it aloud. "Just familiar things in general. Letting go is a part of growing up."

Clay looked at her and saw how she was struggling not to say "Khaled", and gently took her hand into his and squeezed it. "The journey of a thousand miles begins with a single step."

*****

Jessica was in her room getting ready to go to Clay's party at Blue Palm Apartments. She was going to wear a red t-shirt, but all of them had "I love Khaled" written on the front. Her mother popped her head around the door when she was looking at the tops and worriedly rubbing her lips.

"I told you! You shouldn't have gotten that statement written across all your tops."

"Not all of them," Jessica said to her, "just the red ones, because red is Khaled's favorite color."

Her mother came into the room fully and leaned on the wall. "You must introduce us to Clay. The whole family wants to meet him."

"Why?" Jessica asked frowning.

"Because he is a miracle worker." Kylie came into the room. Her pregnant belly looked like it was going to pop at any moment. She waddled to the side of Jessica's bed and sat down.

"What are you doing here?" Jessica asked.

"I heard through the family grapevine that you have a new guy," Kylie said, "and you are going out on a date. I had to come see this."

"He's not picking me up here," Jessica said in relief. "I am driving to the Blue Palm Apartments to see him. You guys are acting like this is my first date."

"Technically, it is," her father said from the doorway. He came and stood beside her mother. "Why can't this Clay come and pick you up?"

Jessica groaned. "It was a casual offer to go to his block party. He is just a friend."

"Whom you like very much," Kylie said. "I can't recall a time, in recent history, that I have come into your room and it was blissfully silent. Khaled is gone and Clay is in, a real live male who we can speak to and get to know. Jessica has a real live boyfriend; what a relief."

Jessica put her head in her hand, "I wasn't that bad was I?"

"Yes, you were," her mother and her sister said at the same time.

Her father just nodded. "I must say that I am feeling relieved, so relieved that I may forgo investigating Clay, at least until I meet him."

Jessica grinned. "Oh, yippee! Heard that Kylie? I must be the only child who is going on a date with somebody that Dad hasn't had investigated."

"Just for now," her father said grinning. "Bring him to

meet us soon before I get too curious."

Jessica rolled her eyes and glanced at the watch. "It is not a given that Clay and I will get serious you know. I think you guys are way too happy about one little outing."

Her mother laughed. "No, I think we are right about this one. Let's get out of her hair," Celeste said, taking Bancroft's hand, "and let her get dressed."

When they left, Kylie reclined on the bed. "Don't expect me to move; I am in a very good spot here on your bed and moving is too much of a bother."

Jessica shook her head. "What should I wear instead of red?"

She chose an orange top instead and pulled her hair into a low chignon, allowing a few tendrils of her curls to linger around her face.

Everybody had pronounced her gorgeous when she left the house, and she drove up to Blue Palm Apartments feeling only slightly nervous. She got out of the car and knocked on the door of apartment 1B.

Clay answered promptly, his eyes widening when he saw her. "Wow. You look super pretty."

Jessica grinned. "Thanks. It's seven forty. Sorry I am so early, but I didn't want to stay at home one minute more. My family was going into a tizzy just because I am going out with a real guy."

Clay grinned. "You are most welcome to come early. Come on in."

He opened the door wider and she entered. He had on a white top and black jeans, and the apartment smelled of his cologne. It was a woodsy scent. She liked it. She liked him. Her eyes ran over him appreciatively. He was playing a CD. It was the acoustic version of one of Khaled's CDs; it was a gospel hymn compilation. The song that was playing was

Precious Memories.

"I've never heard that one before, I mean the acoustic version. His voice sounds so pure here without all the instruments to drown him out," Jessica said in awe.

Clay looked at her closely. "I am not reawakening any addictions, am I?"

"No," Jessica laughed uncomfortably. "I am not addicted to Khaled." After taking a breath she asked, "Can I borrow this CD? I mean, it must be the only one I don't have."

Clay sighed. "You can have it."

Jessica grinned. "Thank you so much. Are you sure?"

Clay nodded. "Yes. There is more where that came from."

Jessica sat down. Clay had not messed with the standard decoration of the Blue Palm complex. He added a model ship to the center table and there was a picture of him with two middle-aged persons standing near an oceanfront.

"Who are they?" Jessica asked.

"My parents," Clay said. "It was one of those rare times when my Dad came back from the cruise ship and spent almost six months at home. That was ten years ago."

"What does your mom do?" Jessica asked.

"She's a florist. She owns a shop back home in Kingston. When I was younger, I had to help out in the shop, so I appreciated the beauty of flowers and I started writing poetry. I used to play football just to balance it out, you know."

"Oh." Jessica smiled. "You were teased because you were sensitive?"

Clay nodded. "I was geek personified. My favorite place was always at the back of the library."

"It's funny," Jessica said grinning. "You don't look like any geek I know."

Clay sat beside her and then jumped up. He was not having just friendly feelings for Jessica. He wanted to put his hand on her shoulder and draw her closer to him just now. "Ready?"

"Sure," Jessica said, standing up.

When she and Clay entered the pool area, there were a few people milling around. Tracy Carr walked up to them, a wide smile on her face that dimmed somewhat when she looked at Jessica.

"Hello, Clay. I am happy that you could join us, and with a date too, how nice."

"Hi, Tracy, this is Jessica, my friend. Jessica, Tracy is my neighbor and she is the one who told me about the party."

Jessica shook Tracy's outstretched hand and almost shuddered at the cold look in her eyes.

"You are Presidents Bancroft's daughter?" Tracy asked. The smile she had plastered on her face not even near her frigid eyes.

"Yes," Jessica nodded, "I am."

"Well, well," Tracy said, "it's a pleasure to have Mount Faith royalty among us. Enjoy yourselves." She turned to Clay. "Good to see you again."

Clay nodded.

"She was cold," Jessica said when Tracy walked off. "Ironically, I think she was my cousin Arnella's friend. I don't know why they stopped talking though."

Clay shrugged. "I get the feeling that Tracy rubs people the wrong way. She is my lab partner's girlfriend though, and he is going crazy over her."

Jessica chuckled. "She seems like a femme fatal, keep out of her way."

"I will," Clay looked at her seriously. "There is only one girl's way I want to be in right now."

Jessica swallowed, and they stared at each other, only breaking eye contact when a bright voice said to them. "Excuse me, my name is Sydney; I am new here. Who are you guys?"

They had to mingle with other people, but even when they were separated and were chatting in different groups, Jessica could feel their connection. She liked that; she liked it a lot.

Chapter Five

Jessica was having a rare bad day on the Monday after her Saturday night out with Clay. She was stuck in Music Room 3 with a slow learner. She was teaching her lone student to play the piano, and it was trying her patience. She glanced at the clock periodically, waiting for the hour to be up.

She was doing a minor in Music Education and had to teach an instrument for seven hours per week. She had chosen the piano as her instrument; after all, she had learned to play it when she was just four years old. As result, she thought that teaching it would be a walk in the park.

Her students were the ones who assessed her after each session. She glanced at the questionnaire on the desk behind her and sighed. She wanted to graduate next year, so she just had to grin and bear it. Though she wanted to wring the neck of her current student, she was smiling with him vaguely as he banged out the most tuneless sound ever to come from the piano.

She had told him time and time again that he was doing it the wrong way, but he refused to listen. She closed her eyes and imagined that the timeless Beethoven's "Fur Elise" was playing instead of the garbled nonsense her student was torturing her with.

Inevitably, she thought about Clay when she closed her eyes. Since Saturday night, he had been on her mind constantly. She found herself thinking about him at the oddest moments and smiling to herself.

She had watched him in action on Saturday night—calm and cool. He was the guy everyone wanted to talk to, and he didn't even do anything to invite the attention. People just liked him. Women just liked him, she corrected. All of the Block 1 women had been buzzing around him like he was the center of a hive, especially that Tracy Carr. She had found an excuse to speak with him at every turn, and Clay had handled the attention with equanimity.

He was mature and wasn't overwhelmed by the attention. Jessica liked that—his maturity and his smile. He had a way of smiling slowly; it started with a small upturn of his lips and then it slowly spread across his chiseled lips and moved to his eyes. It lit her up inside. She was a goner for sure, but then she had the worrying thought that she was probably too immature for Clay.

Maybe she needed to tone down her youthful exuberance. What did Ramon call her—a livewire?

She was forcibly dragged out of her reverie when her student ended the piece on a maddening crescendo. She cupped her ears.

"That's the most ear auditory abuse I've gotten in a while."

Her student looked at her, a frown marring his brow. Jessica looked at his name badge. His name was Ronald.

"Is that good or bad?" he demanded.

Jessica opened her eyes wider. "It depends on if you like auditory abuse."

"Huh?" He got up from around the piano and hissed his teeth. "Where's the evaluation sheet?"

"Over there." Jessica pointed at the stack of papers on the table and glanced at her watch; it was a Khaled limited edition timepiece with Khaled's face in the middle. She looked at his face and it failed to raise a smile out of her. She was really moving on.

She studied him as she heard Ronald scribbling his evaluation. He had a smooth caramel complexion, shiny curly hair—some of it was in his face. He had green eyes and extremely white teeth.

Deidra always teased her that Khaled looked too pretty. She had to agree now. She had never really seen it before. To even think it was being disloyal to him. She looked at him, comparing him to Clay's more manly, rugged features.

She jumped when Ronald slapped down the evaluation on the desk and walked out of the room without telling her goodbye.

Ungrateful, she thought, feeling amused: after he had abused her ears, he had the audacity to walk out on her.

She got up and picked up her backpack. She loved teaching music, but teaching Ronald made one thing clear to her: she would much rather work with children; they grasped the concepts faster and handled the instruments with more adeptness than adults.

She had to face it; she might have to end up teaching music unless she was going to open her own recording studio. It would be nice to open a studio with Clay. The thought flitted across her mind and she shoved it back. He was doing chemistry. He wasn't interested in the studio life anymore.

She had it in the back of her mind to ask him to give her

a tour of his uncle's studio, but she didn't want him to think she was asking because she wanted to meet Khaled in person. She did, but that was not why she was interested in Clay.

She walked to the porch of the building and realized that outside was prematurely dark even though it was just five-thirty. It was going to rain. The dark ominous clouds in the distance looked like they were going to burst any second now.

She wished she had driven to school instead of taking the ten-minute walk over. Now she, her bag, and the evaluation sheet were going to be soaked. Maybe her evaluation by Ronald could do with a good soaking; she wouldn't mind.

She had to call someone to come and pick her up. She took out her phone, and her hands hovered over Ramon's name. She scrolled through her contacts list and called Clay instead. She wanted to see him. Why not?

He answered on the first ring. "Jessica?" His smooth, honey voice calling her name almost had her stammering.

"Can you come pick me up?" Jessica asked, "I didn't drive this morning."

"Sure. Where are you?" he asked eagerly.

She smiled after she hung up. He didn't even hesitate. He liked her all right.

*****

Clay drove up in a black Range Rover. Jessica's eyes widened; she had no idea that he drove such a luxurious vehicle. As soon as she slammed the door behind her, the first splatter of rain hit the windshield. "You reached here in record time," she grinned at Clay.

Clay nodded. "And at the right time too. It is going to be a wet night." He wiped away a wet spot that was on her cheek.

"You look gorgeous, you know that?"

Jessica flushed. It was the almost fortuitous Smoky Robinson's song, Cruisin', that came on the radio at that moment. She couldn't keep eye contact with him; his stare was so intense. Jessica started humming along to the song.

Clay looked through the windshield. "Where do you want us to cruise to?"

"I was thinking to my home." Jessica put on her seatbelt. Her day, which had seemed as slow as molasses, was now brighter. The rain was coming down in earnest now, and they could barely see through the downpour in front of them.

"Or we could wait for the rain to subside and then head to Alligator Pond and eat fish on the beach," Clay said.

Jessica nodded vigorously. "That would be great."

Clay grinned. "I have been wanting to do that ever since I moved here in the summer. I hadn't found anybody to go with whose company I would enjoy, until now."

Jessica smiled. "I am willing to go on any new adventure with you...er... that is if you want to."

Clay looked at her. The rain on the glass was creating patterns where the shadow hit his face. "I want to."

They watched as the rain drove against the glass like a silvery sheet. Clay turned on the heater in the car and they listened to the old hits playing on the radio. It felt as if they were in a comfortable cocoon. Jessica loved the feeling. She wondered if Clay was thinking the same.

"Can you sing?" Jessica asked him after a short silence.

Clay smiled. "I'd rather not say."

Jessica grinned. "Your voice can't be that bad."

"It's not." Clay looked at her. He opened his mouth to say something and then stopped.

"Your voice sounds like it would make a lovely tenor," Jessica said helpfully.

Clay laughed. "Thank God you didn't say soprano."

Jessica chuckled. "Why did you break up with your last girlfriend?"

Clay turned around in the seat and looked at her in the half-dark. "That's a very creative way of asking if I have a girlfriend."

Jessica nodded. "So, why?"

"It was a year ago. She migrated to Canada."

"That's it?" Jessica asked, feeling jealous of the faceless, nameless girl.

"That's it." Clay shrugged. "It was without fireworks or fanfare. She called from the airport and told me sayonara. Literally. She said, Clay I am leaving you, sayonara."

"Khaled sang a song about that," Jessica said eagerly. "Sayonara to Kara, no tears, just cheers, don't worry I know that you are sorry."

"I wrote that," Clay said simply. "And yes, her name was Kara."

"You write songs for Khaled?" Jessica asked in awe. "Why didn't you say something?"

"It's no biggie." Clay shrugged. "When you are at a studio and you write poems, all you have to do is put music to them and have a decent hook, voila a song is born."

Jessica moved closer to see his eyes in the dark. "No biggie? I thought Khaled wrote all his songs."

Clay shook his head. "No! I don't think he wrote any of his songs."

Jessica was itching to ask Clay a million and one questions, but she could see from his response that he was reluctant to talk about Khaled. There was just something in the way he tensed up when she mentioned the singer. What was it that Clay knew about Khaled? He always answered any Khaled questions cagily.

The song "Just To See Her" by Smokey Robinson came on and Clay looked at her. "Now that's my favorite song. I love the lyrics and his voice."

Jessica nodded. "I like it too. I think Khaled should do a cover of it."

"He's retired, remember?" The rain was easing up slowly and Clay looked out. "Still want to go with me to the seaside? This doesn't feel like seaside weather."

"Most definitely want to go." Jessica nodded.

*****

The rain had stopped by the time they reached the town of Junction, and it had not even touched Alligator Pond, where they were heading. The night was pitch dark on the road leading to the location, and the air felt muggy. As they turned toward the sleepy fishing village, Jessica could smell the sea, which she knew was not far from where they were.

"I am really looking forward to this," Jessica said excitedly. "The sea always excites me."

"That's because Mount Faith is so landlocked." Clay replied.

He glanced at Jessica's brown sparkling eyes and smiled. Jessica was interesting company. She laughed with gusto, sang when a particular favorite song of hers came on the radio, and she was completely uninhibited and fun. He needed a little of that in his life.

He wondered when in the last few years he had been around anyone who made him feel so comfortable and happy at the same time. He really liked Jessica's approach to life; it made him feel carefree again, a feeling he hadn't felt for years.

As if to underscore the futility of his latest thoughts, his cell phone rang. He answered as he drove up to the popular

Little Ochi Restaurant, which was right on the beach; there were quaint little thatch-roof huts that were fashioned out of canoes. He had been admiring them when he answered his phone without looking on the call display. He was almost sorry that he did.

"So you are alive?" Noel Reid asked.

"I am." Clay glanced at Jessica. She was looking at him, an easy smile on her face. "Now is not the time, Uncle Noel," he hissed. "I am on a date."

"Clay, we are in trouble! The stupid boy is about to destroy the brand."

"Which boy?" Clay asked.

"Don't act dumb," Noel hissed. "You know who. He has gone and decided to court trouble. Six years of managing him and managing the media carefully and he decides to give a tell all interview."

"Run that by me again," Clay said quietly.

"According to him, he is retired." Noel snorted, "Now he can do what he wants, just like you did. You started this Clay. You know he has always copied everything you do. I wanted one more album and this is what happens. This is your fault."

"And you were too greedy," Clay said. "I have to go."

"Don't you dare leave me to handle this fall out alone," Noel groaned. "We have to come up with a plan. This is just as much your business as it is mine."

"This whole thing was your idea," Clay said calmly. "Maybe it's time somebody did a tell all. Nothing stays hidden forever. Khaled is really retired. No more albums." He hung up and looked across at Jessica, whose mouth was wide open.

She closed it hurriedly.

"Well, I couldn't help overhearing. It would have been

awkward for me to leave the car and just stare into thin air," she said faintly.

Clay nodded. "Yes. Let's go eat. I am famished, and these people make the best fried fish this side of Jamaica."

He saw the curiosity in her eyes, but he couldn't bring himself to answer her or give her an explanation though he knew she was dying to have one.

He got out of the car, and Jessica followed him. "Are you serious? You mentioned Khaled over the phone to your uncle and had a totally cryptic conversation and then you just say 'let's go eat.'"

She was feverishly taking off her shoes to walk in the sand. Clay sighed. He had to give her something or he suspected that he would not be hearing the end of it all night.

He took off his shoes as well, all the while contemplating what he should say to her. He settled on, "It's just the inner workings of a studio. My greedy uncle is just facing some issues stemming from some creative decisions he made a long time ago."

"So what about Khaled?" Jessica asked, confused more than ever at his reply. "Why are you so insistent that he is retired."

"My uncle wanted another album from him, but Khaled is retired and staying that way, and I can't help my uncle at the studio at the moment. I need a break." Clay sighed. "Hey, Jess, were you serious about growing up and growing out Khaled?"

Jessica stopped walking. They had both been heading toward the sea instead of to the restaurant. She nodded. "Well, I am trying to. I really am."

"Good." Clay took her hand in his. "It's the here and now that really matters, and the real."

Jessica swallowed. "And what is it that's real?"

"The sand under your toes, the warm sea water lapping the side of the shore. My hand in yours." He hugged her to him, and they stayed like that for a long while, watching the dark sea.

Chapter Six

Clay walked into the science lab on Tuesday morning, earlier than usual, with his phone jammed firmly to his ear. His uncle was in full panic mode.

"The Jamaican Insider is going to carry the story and the fool is going to be doing a tell all interview with Michelle Sommers on Channel 4." Neil Reid sounded like he was going to cry. "She is ruthless; she has chewed up and spat out more formidable people than Khaled."

Clay chuckled and sat down at the front of the lab. He waved to Stewart, who was already there. Obviously, he was not the only one who was off to an early start. Ray was there as well and had set up the ingredients to make the gunpowder on his table as a demonstration.

Stewart frowned at Clay and called him over to their regular table. Clay shook his head and held up his finger. He didn't want Stewart to hear the conversation that he was having with his uncle.

He folded his arms and tried to talk to his uncle sternly. Their roles were now well and truly reversed. His uncle, his father's eldest brother, was the father figure in his life and the one who Clay had relied on for advice, but he was now asking Clay for advice. He wondered if he should be finding the situation as funny as he was. He learned a long time ago that nothing really lasted forever. The last few years with Khaled were profitable for them, but all good things must end eventually.

He really hoped that Khaled did not tell all, as he was threatening to do. If he did, he would have a huge legal battle on his hands. They had all signed a confidentiality agreement, which would not expire for at least another year. The contract had a seven-year term; until that time elapsed there should be no revealing of the inner workings of the iJam studio. He figured his uncle was now regretting that the contract period wasn't longer.

"Khaled can't tell all," he reminded his uncle after the older man had gone into a heavy silence.

"Why on earth not?" His uncle asked, pained. "I always knew that boy was as dumb as a doorknob. If he can't interpret the contract, he'll tell all right."

Clay chuckled. "We've always known that one day something like this would happen. Let's hope that is not too damaging."

His uncle sighed. "At any rate I have PR working on a slant to this whole thing just in case that moron goes on national television un-coached and ruins everything."

"What about your best of Khaled album?" Clay asked.

"I have to scrap the release date until the talk that this interview is going to generate dies down. Maybe I can't release it for years."

"Or maybe you could come clean and have this whole

thing straightened out," Clay said, probing to see if his uncle was willing to tell the truth to the world.

"No," His uncle said abruptly. "Not yet. I'll have to hear what 'Dumbo' says in the interview before I do anything."

Clay said contemplatively, "This is all your doing, you know, your brilliant idea."

"Yes," Noel said, "but don't kick a man when he's down. Saying 'I told you so' won't help me at this time. I always come up with something." He paused and then he asked. "How was your date last night? What's her name?"

"Jessica," Clay said lightly. "It was a great date. I like her."

"I hope we don't have another Kara on our hands," his uncle said heavily. "She used you to get close to Khaled, remember. When that oddball messed with her mind and promised her forever she dumped you."

"How could I forget?" Clay murmured. The sorrow he had felt after that event was no longer there. "Jessica is nothing like Kara."

His uncle snorted, "Well, I doubt she will want to be near Khaled when he does this tell all interview."

"When is it going to be aired?" Clay asked. Even though he was not as anxious as his uncle to hear what Khaled was going to say in the interview, he felt a bit apprehensive. Maybe he should watch it with Jessica. She would probably feel the most put out by the revelations.

He hung up the phone and glanced on the table where Ray had spread out his gunpowder ingredients. On the table, he had what looked like ground sugar beside the charcoal. That made sense. In times past, ground sugar was used to make gunpowder as well. He could see that this was going to be an interesting class. He glanced at his watch; class would start in five minutes. More students had trickled in while he was on the phone. He looked over at Stewart who was busily grinding an ingredient with a small mortar.

He went over to the table and said to his lab mate. "You are here early."

Stewart grunted. "I am. So what?"

"Nothing, nothing." Clay held up his hand. Stewart sounded hostile. "I see that Ray is going to use sugar instead of charcoal."

"It can be used. Sugar is good fuel," Stewart mumbled, "Niter and saltpeter are good oxidizers. That nerd thinks he is the only one who can make gunpowder. I have been doing this since I was a little boy. I can't believe they teach this in university and you get a grade for it."

Clay nodded. He didn't want to roil Stewart up because he looked like he was angry enough to explode. When Ray entered the class he looked excited. "I got sandbags and permission from the school heritage board to use the old blunderbuss that is displayed in the historical room. It is two hundred years old."

A young guy with a sullen expression came through the door with the old gun; holding it carefully and inspecting it as Ray gestured to it.

"The blunderbuss is a close range weapon. In the past some fired a very large ball. Most were loaded with a cluster of pistol balls, nails, glass, or just about anything else that was in good supply."

Ray licked his lips. "It was very deadly and weighed between ten and sixteen pounds. This one weighs twelve pounds and is two feet in length. Back then, this was considered small, especially among pirates. It has a large barrel," he pointed to the barrel, "and a bore diameter of around two inches. The barrel is flared outward at the end like a funnel. It was fashioned this way so that it could do a lot of close range damage. I think this gun precedes the musket and was used by plantation owners in these parts."

"Are you sure that it can be safely fired?" one of the guys asked doubtfully. "It looks heavy and rusty."

"It is heavy and rusty, but we are going to build gunpowder and try it." Ray was almost salivating. "Today we are going to make history and science come alive. The person who makes gunpowder that can propel the shot will get an 'A' for this lab."

The guys were grinning with glee, and the girls were looking doubtfully at the big black rusty thing.

"Oh, one more thing," Ray said. "We will not be using anything too dangerous, as they did in the past. We are going to wrap potatoes in cloth and use them as projectiles. The gunpowder is supposed to go into the barrel before the potato is put in. We'll wrap the powder in very thin cloth and light it—real primitive but there is a science lesson here."

"Thank God for that." One of the girls said feelingly.

"But," Ray held up his finger, "a small sack of potato can sting if it is propelled hard enough, and we are dealing with gunpowder. So please, follow the precautions I am now going to hand out to you."

Stewart was grunting all through Ray's talk, and Clay looked at the powder he was grinding. "That is very finely grounded," he said to Stewart.

"The finer the powder, the better it works. Didn't you hear when the twerp said that?"

"Why do you sound so mad with me?" Clay asked.

"Because you are sleeping with her too." Stewart hissed. "I saw you talking and smiling with her at that little bonfire party on Saturday night. All the girls were coming onto you because you were playing like you were Mr. Cool."

"Who is this her that you are talking about?" Clay asked slowly.

"Tracy," Stewart said, seething. "Don't pretend as if you don't know who I am talking about."

Clay frowned. "She is my neighbor. We live on the same block. I went to the block party with Jessica Bancroft. She is the girl that I like."

"You are a real player aren't you?" Stewart said, his eyes looking a little crazy. "Jessica is Ramon's girl."

"No, she's not. They are just friends." Clay rubbed his neck. "Look Stewart, maybe you should stop assuming things about me and Ray and Tracy."

"So you are friends with Ray too, huh?" Stewart growled. "What sort of kinky things are you two doing to my girl?"

Clay was exasperated. "Maybe you should talk to your girl about this?"

Stewart sighed, an icy smile creeping across his face. "You are right. I am over- thinking things, too jealous for my own good. I should calm down."

Clay nodded glad that Stewart was seeing sense.

"Okay," Ray said at the top of the class, cutting into the tense little dialogue, "after you have grounded your individual ingredients in the mortar with the pestle, I want you to carefully ground all the ingredients together. Please follow all the steps on the paper to avoid any accidents. I want to see a sample under the microscope to make sure that it is good enough. I am giving you ten minutes with it."

Clay was carefully grinding his powders together as instructed when Stewart touched him with his goggles on.

"Want to see how fine my powder is?" He indicated to the microscope. "It seems that all you need is a little anger to grind the ingredients to a real fine powder."

Clay looked at him distrustfully, this guy seesaws between extreme emotions like a chameleon changes its color.

"Okay," he got up from his seat and looked into the

microscope. The powder was indeed fine, like dust. Stewart must have been really angry.

He was just about to lift up his head when he saw a flash of light and the powder exploded with a sharp bang, sending the acrid black powder into his eyes and nostrils. He held up his head and he could see spot of lights swimming around behind his eyelids.

"Serve you right," he heard Stewart snicker. "Players get what they deserve."

Clay stumbled to his chair. He had a bad taste in his throat. It was as if the powder had gotten into his throat through his nostrils and was stinging him unbearably.

"What happened here?" Ray asked Clay.

Clay could hear Stewart chuckling, "Just Clay playing with fire."

"Are you okay, Clay?" Ray asked.

Clay felt his touch on his shoulder, but he couldn't make him out. There were still circles swimming around behind his eyes.

He coughed, and he heard Ramon's voice.

"Hey, Clay. Can you see me?"

Clay looked in the direction of his voice. There was nothing, just a shadowy outline, and those annoying shapes running behind his eyelids. "No," he said faintly.

"Oh, my God!" Ray said. "You idiot! You lit the gunpowder when he was looking into the microscope. Are you crazy?"

Clay heard someone on their phone, and after a brief moment, he could hear and feel students ebbing and flowing around him. He was coughing intermittently. His whole face felt like it was stinging him.

He felt the gentle hand of a lady on his shoulders. All the time he was struggling to breathe.

"Clay Reid. I am Nurse Coreen. I am going to accompany

you to the Medical Center."

*****

"Clay, I am Dr. Henry Grime. Please indicate with a nod that you are hearing me."

Clay nodded. He had been having a panicky few hours with a million and one faceless people scurrying around him. Now and again someone would tell him that it was going to be okay, but how would it be okay when he couldn't even see?

He had finally stopped coughing, and a Nurse Dennis had given him nose drops. It was still stinging him, as if he had the flu and had been sneezing too hard and too long. His nose and throat area felt sore. Now he assumed that he was in an office because it was quiet, and he could hear the rustle of papers. He was blanketed behind a wall of stifling darkness. His right eye could barely make out brown shapes, but his left eye was completely dark. He squeezed the handle of the chair that he was sitting in and waited for this Dr. Henry Grime to speak again.

"I am going to be doing an examination of your eyes."

Clay nodded. His throat felt scratchy and abused when he opened his mouth. "I can't see anything from my left eye." His voice was hoarse and sounded gravelly to his own ears.

"Yes. That was the eye that got a direct hit." Dr. Grime said gently.

"This feels unreal," Clay said. "Am I going to be blinded forever or something?" He couldn't stop the panic from lacing his voice.

"No. I doubt that." Dr. Grimes said confidently. "I am preempting myself. Let me examine your eyes first."

He came around to Clay's side of the table. Clay felt his

presence, but he had no idea what he was doing. He realized how much of a privilege having one's sight is. He felt extremely vulnerable behind his veil of darkness. Tears were building up but he willed himself not to cry. He wasn't a baby, but he was afraid. The tears were stinging his eyes though.

The doctor said to him, "Tears are actually cleansing, and at least I know that your tear ducts are working." He gave Clay a bundle of tissue and excused himself from the office. It was the first time in his life that Clay was feeling so utterly lonely and bereft and the tears did roll down his cheeks. They felt hot and they stung. He dabbed his eyes and wondered if his tears were black like the powder that exploded in his eyes. He didn't even hear when the door to the office opened.

"Oh, Clay." A warm body engulfed him. The person had ample cleavage that was pushing into his back, so he knew it was not Jessica; she was not as well endowed. The shaft of disappointment he felt was overwhelming.

"I came as soon as I heard." he recognized the voice now. It was Tracy Carr.

"I can't believe how out of control Stewart has gotten. When we broke up a few weeks ago I had no idea that he would become unhinged. If it makes you feel better," her hair was tickling the side of his face. It smelled like strawberry. "The police have taken him into custody. Apparently, he's been threatening Ray too. Ray has been helping me with a project for a stupid science subject I flunked last semester."

Clay sighed. "Yes, he's out of control."

"I know." Tracy was rubbing his hand. "I heard that you can't see."

Clay nodded.

"So you can't see the green skirt suit I am in right now?" Tracy asked, almost disappointed.

Clay shook his head. "Sorry."

The door opened again, and the doctor cleared his throat. "Miss, you will have to wait outside like the rest of Mr. Reid's friends."

"There are people waiting outside?" Clay asked faintly.

"Yes. Loads of them," the doctor said. The door closed behind Tracy. "Now that your eyes have had a cleansing bath, let's examine you."

He held up Clays left eyelid and then his right.

"When you say there are people outside waiting for me, is Jessica Bancroft out there?" Clay asked eagerly.

"A pretty girl with brown hair and a tearful face? Yes, she's the most anxious to see you." The doctor said gently.

"Thank you," Clay said with a grateful sigh.

"No problem," The doctor said. "Can you see this?"

"What?" Clay asked.

"So you can't see it."

"Lean forward." When Clay leaned forward he could see a faint light from his right eye.

He told the doctor, who said softly, "That's good." After several more tests, Dr. Grime went back to his side of the desk. Clay heard the ruffling of several papers before he spoke.

"The good news is your right eye is not severely damaged. The bad news is your left eye is badly bruised from those particles and you may be getting some reaction from the potassium nitrate—runny, stinging eyes and sensitivity to light. I will assess your eyes again in a few days; maybe by then your sight will be back. I don't anticipate that both eyes are permanently damaged. Until then, I have a prescription for you. It is a solution to drop in your eyes twice per day. I assume from observing that anxious young woman outside that you will have support during this very scary time of your life?"

"I guess so," Clay said, relief flooding his voice.

*****

"We are not going to invite that boy to stay with us," Ryan Bancroft hissed into the phone. "Jessica likes him. She is my baby girl, and he is an older man. It is a recipe for disaster."

"He is blind," Celeste said calmly. "We can't have him living alone."

"Lots of blind people do it," Bancroft said sullenly. "The guest room is too near to Jessica's room. Do you want a repeat of Adrian and Cathy on our hands?"

"Cathy never stayed here," Celeste said.

"Not that we know of," Bancroft said, looking back at the boardroom. He had left a meeting to deal with this latest drama in his family's life. The big wigs were in the boardroom trying not to listen to his conversation. Bancroft grunted at the thought of them doing so.

Young people can find creative ways to get together. He didn't want to literally hand them the keys to do it, and worst yet, do it in his house.

Celeste sighed. "I already told Jessica that he can stay with us for a few days. He can have Deidra's room."

"Deidra's room!" Bancroft hissed. "Don't you think that something is wrong with us? We put up our children's prospective partners under one pretext or the other. It's becoming a pattern, and I don't know anything about this Clay Reid."

"Then find out," Celeste said sweetly. "I already changed the sheets and I asked Adrian to get his bags. He is upset, disoriented, and blind. Let your Christian charity rule instead of your dirty mind."

Bancroft hissed his teeth when his wife hung up and wondered why she bothered to called and tell him about this Clay boy staying at the house anyway. She knows who really runs the house.

He straightened his spine and headed to the boardroom. At least there he had some power.

Chapter Seven

"**D**o you want me to get you anything?" Celeste Bancroft asked Clay every ten seconds. He was still trying to figure out how he was ensconced in the Bancroft's living room and why he allowed himself to be railroaded into staying with the family of the university's president.

He remembered Jessica's warm tears on his neck when he was led out of the doctor's office. Feeling disoriented, he remembered her feverishly saying that she would take care of everything and Ramon saying that he would be his eye for the rest of the semester if he wanted.

He couldn't fathom why he had given in like he had, but he had to face things. He was torn from everything that was familiar, and he was grateful for the Bancroft's help.

Jessica was sitting beside him now, holding his hands. Earlier she had told him where everything was and had gone into great detail about the layout of the house. Mrs. Bancroft had told him to call her Celeste.

He was beginning to feel smothered, and blind. This was a hard blow for someone who was very much used to depending on his sight. Now he was waiting for his other senses to kick in.

"Okay, I am going to leave you two alone now," Celeste said in her gentle maternal voice. "You can sort out what you are going to do next, Clay." That reminded him that he had to call his own mother and tell her about this latest development in his life, or maybe not.

"I can't believe this happened to you. Why would Stewart do such a thing?" Jessica said to him, her hands moving gently over his.

"He said that he saw me talking to Tracy on Saturday night at the bonfire thing, and he said I stole you from Ramon."

"Ridiculous!" Jessica's hands jerked on his, and he held them steady. She was nervous. He could feel her pulse under her skin.

"Is everything okay?" he asked softly.

"No," Jessica growled, "I am quite nervy on your behalf. Stewart is telling everybody that he had no idea that the lighter in his hand would give off a spark and that he had nothing against you. I don't believe him."

Clay sighed. "I can only think that he is off his meds. He was pretty roiled up with me and with Ray."

"He should be locked up for good." Jessica got up, and he heard the steady pounding of her feet on the floor. She was pacing feverishly. "I can't stand that pinched-face Stewart. Do you see how close set his eyes are? He looks evil."

Clay chuckled. "Oh Jess. Stop being mad on my behalf. I am sure my sight will come back."

"You should sue him," Jessica said, coming to sit beside him again. He felt when the settee shifted and her weight sank the cushion and her soft curves pressed near his hand.

"I am not going to sue him," Clay said. "I am just going to pretend that this is an accident and leave it alone. I am however going to recommend counseling for Stewart. His feelings for Tracy are bordering on being obsessive."

Jessica snorted. "You don't say. Anyway, it's near evening; the sun is peeping through the curtains like a golden swathe on the walls. What do you want to do?"

Clay smiled. "I can picture that. For now, I want to be still. I have a slight headache and a definite throat, ear and nose ache."

"Maybe it's a good idea if you sleep," Jessica said softly. "Maybe when you wake up your vision will be back."

Clay nodded. "I really hope so."

"If not, we are going to have to get you a stick to move around with."

"Or a guide dog," Clay said, trying to be humorous but feeling a sharp sense of panic at the thought of losing his sight forever. He couldn't think that way.

"Well, we have Daryl. He's Daddy's dog, and he only likes Daddy. He tolerates Mommy, and he has a love hate relationship with me."

Clay got up unsteadily, and Jessica stood beside him. "I know how scary this must feel but don't worry, I got your back."

For some reason that made Clay feel like crying. He battled the feeling of vulnerability and held on to her hand as she guided him to a guest room. She sat beside him while he closed his eyes and tried to sleep.

She had only known him for two weeks, but she hadn't run to the hills when she heard that he was blind. She didn't know anything much about him really. She was just being Jessica, kind hearted and sweet.

He fell asleep to her singing one of her favorite Khaled

songs.

*****

"Have you told your family about your situation yet, Clay?" Dr. Bancroft was sitting at the head of the table. Celeste was beside him.

Clay imagined that they were both looking at him curiously. He could barely make out the outline of his head. His right eye was coming back but the progression was extremely slow. Vision from his left eye was still totally black.

He was struggling not to become frustrated, but this was day three. He didn't want to answer Dr. Bancroft. He hadn't told his Mom nor his uncle what was happening, and he had no intention to. His mother would overreact and make him feel worse about the situation, and his uncle was already facing a very stressful situation. Khaled's tell all interview was today. Already, he had called Clay five times since he got up that morning; he was acting so jittery that Clay didn't have the heart to add more bad news to his current situation.

He finally answered Dr. Bancroft. "No, but I have good reason not to."

Dr. Bancroft nodded. "You are waiting until your sight comes back?"

"Yes," Clay said quickly. He may or may not share this story with either his uncle or Mom. Both of them had acted as if coming to Mount Faith was a bad idea: his mother because she wanted to have him closer, his uncle because he wanted help with the final Khaled album.

"Good morning everyone." Jessica breezed into the room. He could smell her perfume: a hint of jasmine. It was scary, but since his sight left, his other senses had indeed sharpened. Celeste smelled faintly of roses. Dr. Bancroft had a fresh clean scent like Brut cologne.

"Good morning," Clay said, looking in her direction. He had taken to wearing dark glasses since they shielded his eyes from bright lights. His doctor said that the sensitivity was a good thing.

Jessica sat beside him, and he couldn't help smiling in her direction. She was always chirpy and full of joy. She squeezed his hand, and he felt her touch long after she had taken her hand away. Two and a half weeks and already he knew that what he felt for this girl was not the usual.

"How are you?" she asked him softly. "Ramon sent over the notes from your classes on tape and the audio book for your chemistry class. He said it was quite easy to find it."

Clay nodded. "I'll thank him later, as well as my lecturers who have been doing the same. I was thinking of returning to classes on Monday. I think I am getting cabin fever."

Dr. Bancroft grunted. "Are you sure you will be able to navigate the campus on your own. Our visually impaired students usually have classes in the special needs block."

Clay cringed. He didn't want to be considered visually impaired. "I will work with Ramon helping me to my classes for now."

"And I'll help you with anything else," Jessica said passionately.

Bancroft cleared his throat and Celeste chuckled.

Clay ate slowly. From early on, he had gotten the hang of eating without help. Celeste had given him a napkin and told him where everything on the plate was. He liked how she treated him. She just told him where stuff was and didn't hover while he learned.

"I have a small issue," a voice said in the room. The person must have walked in softly because Clay did not hear anyone else enter the room. His hand shook and the eggs he had on his fork fell off.

"Sorry if I frightened you," the voice said. "You must be Clay."

Clay nodded in the direction of the voice.

"I am Vanley," the person said. "I hope you get back your sight soon. I know Jess is very excited to take care of you. Anyway, I need your advice Uncle and Aunty."

He walked out of the kitchen. Chairs scraped the floor as both Bancroft and Celeste got up.

"I think he's going to propose to Davia," Jessica said excitedly, "and needs advice from the grays."

"The grays?" Clay asked.

"Yup. That's what I call my parents." Jessica laughed. "Did you know that today is the big Khaled interview? It is going to be aired at three and again at ten, but I am coming home for it at three. Want me to bring lunch for you?"

Clay nodded. "Yes, thanks."

"We'll eat and watch it together," Jessica said. She got up and kissed him on his forehead. Her soft lips left a trail of wetness on his forehead. Clay sat around the table smiling long after she left.

*****

Jessica came home at quarter to three. When she entered the living room, Clay was reclining in the longest settee before the television, which was turned down really low. He lifted his head when the door opened, and she smiled involuntarily. Even with the glasses, half blind, and vulnerable, he was super cute.

"It's me," she said and saw his head relax again. She realized how tough it was on him not to be able to tell who it was that entered a room, but she loved his resilient spirit:

he had not gone into a well of despair. He was being mature about the whole thing.

She sat beside him. "I bought your favorite, chicken patty."

Clay grinned. "Thanks. At least it will make this interview a little better."

"I am so excited about the interview," Jessica said, I can't believe that Khaled, who used to have such an air of mystery about him is going to share himself with the world." She handed him the patty.

"Why don't you look so happy?"

Clay shrugged. "Depends on what he shares. If it's bad it will be catastrophic for my uncle, who is very concerned about the brand."

Jessica turned up the television. The interview had begun. They were playing her favorite Khaled cover 'I Go Crazy'.

"Ooh, it has started on the right note already," Jessica said bouncing up and down on her chair.

Clay just sighed and closed his eyes.

"Today we have with us the notoriously private Khaled, who announced his retirement two short weeks ago, and who is now willing to talk to us unedited."

"Welcome, Khaled."

The interviewer shook his hand, and the camera panned into his face.

Jessica gasped. "He has gotten better looking."

Clay imitated a snore.

"Seriously," Jessica said. "His eyes are so green and his complexion like smooth coco butter."

"Thank you, Michelle," Khaled responded.

"So, the question on everybody's lips these days is why would Khaled, the best-selling voice in the game, retire so suddenly?"

Khaled looked into the television screen. He had cut his

curls, and looked even better than before as a result. Jessica clutched a pillow closely and listened intently. Just a few short weeks ago, she had been devastated to hear of Khaled's retirement.

"I decided to go back to school. Education is important you know. I want this to be an example, especially to my young fans."

"Oh, my," Jessica breathed. "He believes in education."

Clay straightened up in his seat. What was Khaled up to? He wished he could see his face and how he answered the questions.

The interviewer looked bemused. "You are a multimillionaire. Why go back to school?"

"It's something I've always wanted to do, and now it seems like as good time as any. I have six albums under my belt. I have been doing this for years now. I am just taking a hiatus. Maybe when I go back to school I will be inspired, write new material, and come back fresh for the seventh album."

The interviewer was nodding. "So the rumors that you were getting married and starting a family are not true then? At least that was one of the reasons given for your retirement."

Khaled chuckled. His teeth were so white. Jessica was so busy looking at them that she almost missed his answer.

"I can't get married, at least not yet. I haven't found my dream girl."

The interviewer was leaning into him as if she wanted to force him to choose her as his dream girl.

That's because I am your dream girl, Jessica said in her mind. *I've always been.* She wondered which school he was going to attend. She closed her eyes tight and prayed that it was Mount Faith.

Clay was fidgeting beside her uncomfortably.

The interviewer asked a few more questions, and then she

asked. "Your fans are dying to know, is 'Khaled' your real name?"

"No," Khaled said. "My parents gave me the name David. My surname is Green."

"Green like your eyes," the interviewer said breathily. "How appropriate, your surname."

Khaled grinned into the cameras. "Yes. It was like kismet. My eyes and my surname."

"Rubbish!" Clay muttered. "Do people actually believe this soppy, syrupy nonsense?"

"Oh, hush!" Jessica said fiercely.

"Okay we have reached the part in the program where we'll take five questions from fans on our Facebook page. He says he will answer them as truthfully as possible."

The camera zeroed into Khaled and he winked.

"Where's my computer?" Jessica asked anxiously. "I need to ask him which school he is going to attend?"

Clay had an instant headache. "Jessica. I thought you were weaning yourself from Khaled."

"I was. I was," Jessica said, frantically pulling her laptop out of her bag, almost banging it on the edge of the settee in her hurry.

"Okay," The interviewer said. "The first question is from Justine Bent: 'Hi Khaled. I am your fan for life. How did you get started in music?'"

"Ah, good question," Khaled said easily. "I always knew I was born with a musical gene. I went to the famous iJam Studios in Kingston with a tape of myself singing some covers and then Noel Reid, y'all must have heard of the famous Noel Reid, took it from there."

Clay groaned.

"What's the matter with you?" Jessica asked. "That's good publicity for your uncle's studio." She found the program's

Facebook page and typed her question as fast as she could.

"Second question, from Kingsley Taggert," the interviewer asked. "What's the hardest part about being you?"

Khaled paused. "Coming up with my songs. I live to be inspired, but sometimes I get stuck in the inspiration process."

"Hogwash." Clay mumbled. "This is excruciatingly painful for me to listen to."

"Third question, from 'Tia Khaled Is My Guy'. That's a long name." The interviewer chuckled, "If you had to die tomorrow, what would you tell your fans, friends and family?"

Khaled rubbed his chin. "I love you all, my fans. I sometimes feel as if I cannot breathe without you, and that is why I am going to cut my retirement short. To my friends: you all know who you are… don't wear black to my funeral. To my family: you are special bunch of people, and I know you love me."

Clay grunted. "He can't even articulate a heartfelt message to his fans, and this from the guy who writes his own songs."

"Oh, shh," Jessica said, rocking her foot back and forth. "Pick me, pick me."

"Fourth question." The interviewer chuckled. "This one is from Jascinth Timberdale. 'Khaled, will you marry me?'"

Khaled laughed. "Maybe if I knew you, maybe if we meet, maybe if, maybe when, maybe not."

"Good answer," the interviewer said, laughing. "That song, *Maybe,* was from your last album, wasn't it? The album went platinum in a week. I tell you, Khaled, you have an amazing voice. Okay last question, from Jessica Bancroft. *Hi Khaled I am your biggest fan, which school are you planning to go to?"*

Khaled laughed. "I like that name, Jessica. I once dreamt

that I would meet a Jessica who would change my life. I am planning to go to Mount Faith University."

Jessica was shell-shocked. She wanted to squeal, but only a little sound escaped her mouth.

"He is coming here," she whispered in shock. "Did you hear that, Clay. He is coming here and he dreamt that I would change his life."

Clay groaned. His phone rang at the same time. He fumbled for it, wishing with all his heart that he didn't feel so blind and handicapped right at that moment.

"Did you hear that?" His uncle asked when he answered. He could barely hear him over Jessica's hoops and hollers.

"Yes, I heard," Clay said tiredly.

"So that was his plan, to follow you?" His uncle said. "He even knows your girlfriend's name. Clay, he is spying on you. Maybe from the get go. I should send a bodyguard up there just in case he gets any weird ideas in his head."

"No." Clay sighed. "I don't want a bodyguard. I know what Khaled wants."

"Did you tell him that you were going to Mount Faith?"

"Of course not," Clay said tiredly. "I wouldn't have told you either because, believe it or not, you both have a similar way of hounding me."

"I am coming there next week Monday anyway. I have to see you and maybe I'll have a bodyguard discretely watching you."

"No," Clay said weakly.

His uncle hung up and he was left with the sound of Jessica dancing beside him.

"I can't believe it." She was past euphoria. "Clay! When he comes you have to introduce us."

Not over my blind body, Clay thought.

Chapter Eight

"**K**haled is coming to Mount Faith, here, up in the hills, to the school I go to. I can't believe it."

Ramon sighed and looked at Clay, who was fiddling with a walking stick Jessica had gotten him as a present. Clay had a stony expression on his face, and Ramon felt almost sorry for him. He had recently lost his sight, and the girl he likes was now killing him with her Khaled talk. He could remonstrate with Clay. Khaled announcing that he was coming to Mount Faith was something else. He knew that Jessica would be over the moon with excitement.

"Can't you ask President Bancroft when you are around the breakfast table one morning not to let the guy in?" Ramon asked Clay. "He is going to be a big distraction up here. I know several people who will flunk the semester."

He glanced at Jessica, who looked extra pretty today in her earth tone colors. She was wearing her extra large earth tone bracelet that she had made out of shells. That to him spelled trouble. She usually wore it when she was dressing up for some major occasion.

Clay grunted to Ramon's question. His right eye was making out general shapes, but he couldn't make out features clearly: people looked like ghosts, but at least he could see where they were located if they moved their heads or hands. The darkness in his left eye felt as if it had lifted a bit though. It was now more of a pale brown. He had an appointment to see the doctor today, and he was hoping that he would have good news for him.

He couldn't afford to be blind when Khaled made an appearance at Mount Faith. He didn't know what he would get up to. He cursed Stewart afresh in his mind. This whole incident couldn't have come at a worse time.

"Seriously," Ramon said beside him. They were all sitting in the Science conservatory, where most of the science students went to lounge around between classes. "Get the president to block him!"

Jessica looked at Ramon fiercely. "If my Dad does that, I will never forgive him."

Ramon sighed. "And here I was thinking that you had grown out of this fanatic madness and there was hope for you. You are breaking Clay's heart with this Khaled madness."

Jessica was about to heatedly respond, but when she looked at Clay, she realized that she had indeed been going on and on about Khaled, and he had silently listened through her excitement for the last couple of days.

"I...shut up Ramon!" she said guiltily. She gathered her books and was about to stalk off when she remembered that she had promised to take Clay to the doctor.

She sat down and started drumming her fingers on the table.

Ramon smirked at her and mouthed 'serve you right'.

He got up after Jessica glared at him murderously. "Talk to you later, Clay."

When he walked away, Jessica looked at Clay. He was dressed all in black, and had on dark glasses. She couldn't read his expression. He just had his head fixed in one direction. His body was tense though. She could see it in the curve of his fist, and he seemed to be gritting his teeth.

She felt really bad now. She had allowed her youthful exuberance to get the better of her. She had proved to him that all her talk of growing up was just that: talk. Just the very threat of Khaled being in the same space as her was enough for her to forget her resolution.

Jessica cleared her throat. "I am still here, Clay."

"Why?"

"Because I have to take you to the doctor," Jessica said, feeling defensive.

"There is no need to," Clay said, gritting his teeth. "I can take care of myself. I can ask someone else to take me. I don't want to be a burden to you, Jessica."

"You are not a burden," Jessica said exasperatedly. "I like helping you out."

"I don't want to put a damper on your enthusiasm," Clay said. "Your idol is coming to school up here; isn't that what you have always wanted? To be with him. I don't want to get in your way."

Jessica hung her head in shame. "I like doing things for you because I like you, okay. You are not a burden."

Her phone rang and there was a shriek in her ears. "He's here. I just saw him. He's in the admin office. Oh my, Jess. I can't believe it." It was her friend and fellow fanatic, Sabrina.

Jessica cleared her throat. "Sab, find out everything you can, like what his major is going to be, that sort of thing."

"Aren't you coming by?" Sab asked, almost eating her

words in her excitement.

Jessica looked at Clay then clutched the phone tighter. "No. Not now."

She hung up the phone feeling torn, so torn that she had to bite her lip. Khaled was here in the same space as she was and she couldn't follow her natural inclination to run to see him.

She looked at Clay, waiting for the resentment to kick in, but it didn't.

He was giving her a half smile. "That must have been tough."

Jessica grinned and clutched his hand. "You have no idea."

Clay squeezed her fingers in his. "I think I do. Answer me this question, Jess. What is it that makes you so into Khaled, that gives you this feverish, worshipful excitement?"

Jessica closed her eyes. She could vividly remember her first time listening to Khaled. "I was in the bus returning from an economics class school trip in high school and the bus driver turned on the radio and the announcer said, 'and here is a new singer, Khaled. We think he is going to go big with this one.' It was a song about love, loss, and pain. I could hear it coming through in his voice, you know. It was that profound. After that I started searching for his songs, and a face for the voice. The rest his history."

"So you loved his voice and his songs first?" Clay asked quietly.

"Yes," Jessica said. "He has such an amazing voice. I mean…especially in his song 'Loving You', he sounded as if he was crying. I really wanted to be that girl that he was crying over."

Clay said earnestly, "Jess, he is an artist. He was just singing a song. Appreciate him for the art; don't idolize the man. He sings nice songs; his voice is amazing, but he doesn't deserve your worship. Nobody but God does. Please remember that, okay, especially when you meet him in person."

Jessica sniffed. "Okay. Are you only telling me this because you are jealous of Khaled?"

"No," Clay shook his head. "Not jealous of him, not at all. Not even a little bit, but I feel annoyed when I hear you getting excited over him. He is not that special, trust me! I know him."

Jessica tightened her hands in his. "I will try to dampen my excitement."

"Please," Clay said and leaned into the general direction where he saw her outline to kiss her on her forehead but instead, his lips touched hers.

Jessica gasped. Clays lips were soft and hard at the same time, and instead of withdrawing from her when his lips found hers he devoured her mouth with hot compelling urgency, his tongue stabbing between her lips with a piercing sweetness that was as devastating as it was unexpected.

When he raised his head, she was still reeling in her mind. Then she looked around and groaned. There was one lone guy sitting in a corner looking at them knowingly.

Clay cleared his throat. "Sorry."

Jessica touched her lips and whispered, "Don't be."

All thoughts of Khaled were swept into the recesses of her mind with the kiss, her first kiss. Not quite what she had imagined in her fantasies, but it was oh so good.

She grinned at Clay, knowing that he couldn't see, but grinning nontheless. "Ready to go?"

Clay grinned back at her. "Yes, I am ready. I wonder why I am suddenly imagining sunshine."

*****

Neil Reid was waiting in the living room when they returned from the doctor that evening. Celeste had made him tea, and they were talking and laughing.

"So, it's true." Neil looked at his nephew as he gingerly walked into the room with a stick in his right hand, and Jessica clinging to his other hand.

Clay sighed. "Oh, man. I told you not to come here!"

He felt his way to the settee on the left of him and sat down.

"Does your mother know?" Neil demanded.

"No," Clay said sullenly, "and you shouldn't tell her either. This is temporary. The doctor said my eyeballs were scorched. The explosion damaged the light-sensitive membrane that covers the inside of the eyeball, but they are healing at a good pace. Must be all the carrots I had when I was a boy."

Neil didn't even raise a smile. "Who did this?"

"It was an accident," Clay said hurriedly. Last thing he wanted was for his influential uncle to create a scene at Mount Faith.

He couldn't see his expression but he knew he was seething.

"Hi, I am Jessica," Jessica said, holding out her hand to Neil. He was an older, taller, and darker version of Clay. He had a neatly cropped white beard, and he wore a hoop earring in his right ear.

"Hello, Jessica," Neil said. "Pardon my manners. I went to visit your father at his office, and he told me that Clay was living here. I couldn't figure out why he would do that until your mom told me about the accident a few moments ago."

He sat down and looked on Clay again. "Did that boy have anything to do with this?"

"What boy?" Jessica asked curiously.

"Uncle..." Clay said at the same time.

Neil cleared his throat. "Pardon me again. I seem to be feeling very confused and mixed up since Clay's... er... problem."

"That's okay," Celeste said. "Jessica and I will leave you two to talk."

When Celeste and Jessica left the room, Neil asked his nephew again. "How can you be sure that Khaled had nothing to do with this, Clay?"

Clay shrugged. "It was a class accident."

"And you alone were injured?" His uncle asked suspiciously.

"The guy who lit the gunpowder was jealous of me and of everybody. He is a little paranoid about his girlfriend."

"What's his name?"

"Stewart Rhoden," Clay said slowly. "He was my lab partner."

"Is he still in the same class?" Neil asked.

"I think he is still in the same class," Clay said, "but I am not since the incident. I can't see, so I can't do the labs. I have to be graded by theory alone for this class."

"Incident," Neil said tensely. "This incident is too convenient, if you ask me."

"You are paranoid." Clay chuckled. "You sound just as paranoid as Stewart."

Neil snorted. "We'll see about that. Why did Khaled choose Mount Faith University? He knew that you were up here. He is stalking you."

Clay shrugged. "He probably is stalking me, but you created the monster. You tame him."

Neil nodded. "I already had my lawyer call him and warn him about his little stunt with that interview."

"He didn't do any damage," Clay said, reluctantly defending Khaled.

"Because he changed his plans," Neil said. "He decided to conveniently get an education. Today I asked President Bancroft to not let him into the institution, but apparently, the horse is already out of the stable. He applied three weeks ago, under his name David Green, and is now here, ready to start classes. I wonder why that wily old fox decided to come to this particular university. Why now?"

Clay shrugged. "I think you are thinking up a conspiracy where there is none."

Neil shook his head. "In my business, it is good to be paranoid; it has saved my life and help me make good financial decisions more than once."

"So, do you know where Khaled is going to stay?" Clay asked.

"Yes." Neil nodded. "Blue Palm Apartments. I figured that is where you were staying as well, so that is why he got a place there. I think you should stay here with the Bancroft's as long as you can. I don't trust you on the same building with Khaled."

"I am only staying here because I can't see," Clay said. "I really want to get my sight back, so I don't share your sentiments about staying here as long as possible."

"Even though you have that caring, pretty girl here?" his uncle asked slyly.

Clay smiled. "Well, that may be the only reason I stay here."

Neil chuckled. "That's my boy. Now Celeste invited me to dinner, and the president promised to be home in time for it. I am leaving tonight, but only because J Grow, my newest client, is in the middle of recording. I wish you were around, Clay."

"I know," Clay said, "but you promised that you would allow me to take a break without the guilty hounding."

"Okay... okay." Neil rubbed his chin. "But I genuinely miss you back at the stable."

*****

David 'Khaled' Green knew nothing about universities and how they operated. He had signed up for a few courses, most of them at the Performing Arts Building. He especially wanted to learn to play an instrument and had sought out Jessica Bancroft as a tutor.

He had his reasons, and as he entered Music Room 2, where they were supposed to have his very first class, he anticipated seeing her. He really wanted to know who was this girl that Clay Reid found so fascinating. If Clay found somebody fascinating, he did too. He was competitive. Tinges of Kara were forming in his mind. Clay had liked Kara, the petite busty girl with the annoying voice, and he had sought to steal her from him.

It had been too easy, and after he had finished with Kara, she was broken. He had rubbed it into Clay's face that he was the one who could get all the girls if he wanted to, and there was nothing that Clay could do about it.

He almost chuckled in relief when Jessica walked into Music Room 2. He had studied her picture on Facebook. He knew how she looked. He knew she was pretty, and he knew that she was a huge Khaled fan. He saw her mouth opened in an 'O' of surprise, and she looked at him with a dazed expression in her eyes.

Gotcha, David thought. This was going to be too easy, and as he had heard from his sources that this victory would be more painful for Clay than the one with Kara. This one, Jessica Bancroft, would die for him, like so many others.

"Hi," he greeted her with a short wave. He had to keep it

humble. He smiled, knowing his dimple would show.

"I am..."

"Khaled," Jessica breathed, "in the flesh. I can't believe this. Are you my next student?"

David nodded. "Yes, I am. And you must be my instructor?"

"Yes, my name is Jessica. I usually just do introductory classes. You can sign up after the class if you are still interested, and you will get a real teacher. You are supposed to assess my teaching skills. The evaluation forms are over there." She pointed nervously.

"Oh," David smiled at her. "Something tells me that I am going to require you to be my teacher for the long haul."

Jessica's hands were trembling and her voice came out in a squeak. "Me?"

"Yes, why not?"

"I don't think I can do this," Jessica said, feeling surreal. "I mean…you are Khaled! Besides, you know how to play the piano."

"Actually. I don't." Khaled shrugged.

"But you gave an interview in Esquire magazine saying that you play the piano pieces for all your songs, and in your music videos you are always around a piano."

David's mouth tightened and he shrugged. "That was just for the videos and the fans, but see, I am here to learn in order to authenticate things."

Jessica's heart, which was pounding, quieted somewhat. There were so many lies surrounding him and his image. She remembered Clays warning that everything about Khaled was carefully thought out and scripted. It seemed as if his knowing music was also a lie. She felt curiously disappointed. She had hoped that Clay had told her that from a place of jealousy and that the reality would have been gloriously different.

She sighed and then smiled at him. This was still Khaled though. He looked more handsome in person, and more real. His eyes were a hazel green instead of the forest green on magazine covers. His skin looked normal, unlike the photoshopped images that made his skin look smooth beyond real. He really had pink chiseled lips though.

She smiled with him as her nervousness came back, and she tried to prepare herself to teach her famous pupil to play the piano.

Chapter Nine

Clay sat at the back of his Advanced Research Methods class and tried to concentrate on Dr. Hillman's effusive description of the various projects that the final year biochemistry students should anticipate.

The lecture hall was jam-packed. Luckily, Ramon thought of him and saved him a seat. He was becoming indebted to Ramon. He was truly a nice person. If he didn't like Jessica for himself, he would have actively encouraged her not to let such a nice guy slip away from her.

He didn't just like Jessica; he loved her, and that made him uneasy. Whenever he loved, or even remotely liked something, Khaled had always found a way to try to take it from him, and Jessica would make it easy for Khaled by being obsessed over him. Clay thought that she was making progress, but she had been obsessed for years, so a few weeks wouldn't cure her. Yesterday she had come home shell-shocked that Khaled was her teaching practice pupil, but unlike her days of feverish excitement, she had gone silent and contemplative. She even went to her bed early.

Unlike Jessica, Clay wasn't shocked that Khaled had sought her out. Obviously, he had done his research before coming to Mount Faith. He knew exactly where to live: he was living in Apartment 1C, right beside Clay's apartment. The fact that he was doing courses at the Performance Arts Center surprised Clay. He expected him to enroll in the sciences, but now he knew why Khaled was doing the Performing Arts: it was because Jessica did classes there. He would use every opportunity to hurt Clay.

He could lose Jessica. That possibility was very real to him and most likely imminent. He clenched his fist in anger They hadn't known each other for that long, and now he wished that he had approached her at the beginning of the summer when he had just come to Mount Faith, the first day when he saw her at the lab door.

At least he would have been able to leverage time to his advantage. Instead, he was now blind and vulnerable. If Jessica compared him to Khaled, he would be found wanting. He wanted his eyes to heal quickly, but as the doctor had pointed out to him, it would take time.

Maybe by the time it was healed, Jessica would have well and truly forgotten him and succumbed to the dubious charm of David Green. He gritted his teeth, feeling impotent. There were several solutions to his current situation, if he thought hard enough. He could always leave Mount Faith and go back to Kingston. He was sure that Khaled would follow him.

He redoubled his efforts to listen to Dr. Hillman as he reminded himself why he was sitting in class. A year ago, finishing his degree had been so important. He had gotten tired of the same routine and wanted this break. Over the years, he had gotten little time to spend pursuing his interests, so going back to school was his 'me time'. It was unfortunate that neither his uncle nor Khaled had cut him some slack to let him get on with his life as he wanted.

The lecturer's voice penetrated his thoughts. "As you know, central to your final year studies is your research project, which takes up one-third of your final year. For the last couple of classes we have been looking at various research methods. Today, we are offering you the opportunity to join a research group.

Remember, project work does not necessarily mean you have to work in the laboratory. Some students will do computer-based projects, while others may carry out a detailed analysis of research literature in a particular area. The list is right here. You may opt for a laboratory project, a literature review project, or a computing project."

"What do you want to do, man?" Ramon asked him above the buzz of voices around them.

"Literature review." Clay shrugged. "I can't handle much else now."

"Cool. I'll sign us up for that," Ramon said. "I have to put us in the same group so that I can help you."

"Thanks, man," Clay said in Ramon's direction.

"I keep telling you no problem." Ramon laughed. "If it makes you feel better, I am helping you out because you are the one who is going to help me save Jessica from Khaled."

Clay chuckled. "Glad to be of service."

Ramon laughed. "I know."

*****

Clay and Ramon were the last ones to leave the lecture

theatre. Clay had to wait until the mad rush had died down before he could move. Ramon stayed with him.

"You wouldn't guess who is at the door," Ramon said urgently.

"Khaled," Clay said with resignation, "I wondered when he would find me."

"You know him?" Ramon asked incredulously.

"Yes." Clay sighed. "I know him really well."

Ramon was looking at Clay strangely, but Clay couldn't see his speculative expression. Ramon's eyes swung back in the direction of the door.

Khaled was standing there in a forest green long-sleeved shirt to match his eyes, black expensive looking jeans pants, and shoes that looked like they cost as much as a full year's tuition.

Ramon almost shook his head in despair. Clay was no match for this guy. The race was over for Jessica's affections; she would most definitely choose Khaled. He had the looks and the voice that she had been mooning over for years. He watched as Khaled sauntered over to them.

"Hi, I am David Green," he said to Ramon, holding out his hand which had a ring on his pinky finger.

Ramon looked at his hand and reluctantly shook it. The guy was suave and flawless and smelled so good. It was like he was from another planet.

"Hi, Clay," David turned to Clay. "I heard that you are blind. How sad."

Clay grunted, "And curiously, you don't sound sad. What do you want Khaled?"

"I am David up here," Khaled insisted, "just a regular student like everybody else."

Ramon keenly watched the exchange between them.

Clay snarled. "Leave me alone and leave Jessica alone. Go

back to Kingston."

"Jessica," Ramon asked faintly. "He already met Jess?"

Clay sighed. "Yes. He made sure of that."

"Is this Jessica the Jessica who is currently my private music teacher? Such a gorgeous girl. Why are you so protective of her?"

Clay growled. "You could never play the innocent. What do you want?"

"You know what I want," Khaled said, looking at Ramon. "Could you excuse us for a minute? I have unfinished business with Clay here."

Ramon looked at Khaled doubtfully. "I don't know if I should leave. I don't trust you."

"It's okay, Ramon," Clay said. "I am pretty sure the last thing David Green wants to do is kill me or otherwise hurt me."

Ramon nodded. "Okay then, if you are sure. Your next class is at Lecture Room 2. I'll save you a seat."

"Thanks, Ramon," Clay said.

Ramon walked off and Clay heard the squeaking hinges of the lecture theatre door close. He looked in Khaled's direction. He could see his outline: all gray shadows and grains like he was watching a television channel that had a bad reception.

David came near him and leaned close to his ear. "Come back to Kingston, Clay. I need you, at least for another year. Where is your sense of obligation?"

"And I need a break," Clay said, "I want out!"

"A break?" David asked incredulously. "What do you need a break for? You are the behind the scenes person. I am Khaled, and I don't want a break. I love this, Clay. I love my job, and your quitting has made it difficult for me. Just one more album to make it seven," David inhaled, "that's all I ask."

Clay turned his head away from the direction of David's face. "No."

David inhaled sharply. "Okay. Fine. If this is the way you are playing the game."

"This is no game!" Clay said exasperatedly. "I am tired, okay. I just want to finish this degree and when I am done I'll see what's next."

David snorted. "Your little girlfriend, Jessica, calls my name breathily and is nervous when she's around me. I think it's time I put her at ease."

Clay clenched his fist.

"I am going to have her, Clay, your little virginal girlfriend. She's so naive and innocent, very much unlike Kara, who I thoroughly enjoyed." Khaled laughed menacingly. "Did you know that Jessica just loves my songs and she absolutely has never heard another voice as sweet as mine? I put her to bed at nights, Clay."

Clay growled. "If you ever..."

"If I ever touch her, you are going to do what, swat me with your little stick? You can't even see."

Khaled got up and threw Clay's stick away, near to the front of the theatre. Clay heard it landing with a thud.

"Find it now, little blind fella. Find your stick." Khaled taunted.

Clay heard him retreating and sighed heavily. He wouldn't even attempt to go to look for the thing. He would have to feel his way out of the lecture theatre. He got up gingerly in preparation to do so. His heart was beating angrily. He needed to put a stop to this or Jessica could get hurt in the crossfire. After he found his way to the other lecture room and sat down beside a curious Ramon, he was almost convinced that he would have to leave Mount Faith to make this situation go away.

Chapter Ten

Jessica sat in the lotus position in the middle of her bed and was listening to some old music from Khaled's very first album when Clay knocked on her door. She glanced at her clock. It was after ten. He had retired way earlier than usual tonight and had looked unhappy. She jumped up and opened her door.

"Hey. Thought you were sleeping."

"I couldn't sleep," Clay leaned on the door. He was still in the same clothes, except that his shirt was unbuttoned at the top. He had on his dark glasses, so she couldn't see his eyes, but his clothes looked crumpled and he looked worried.

"What's wrong?"

She sat on the bed and watched him as his shoulders slumped.

He listened to the words of the song that was playing; it was a Khaled cover of Phil Colin's, 'Another Day in Paradise'. He smiled slightly. "You know, people don't realize that this is a pretty profound song."

"Yes, about poverty and how we turn a blind eye to it. I know, and Khaled did a great cover," Jessica said. "I love it."

Clay nodded. "I wish I could see. You know, being blind for two weeks is making me appreciate sight. I will never take seeing for granted again."

Jessica cleared her throat. "You have handled it so well though. I know if that happened to me I'd be a panicky mess."

Clay shrugged. "I guess. I am fortunate it wasn't worse and my right eye is slowly coming back."

"Do you want to sit down?" Jessica asked, "or are you okay there, holding up the door."

Clay laughed. "I want to play something. Would your father mind me playing the piano in the living room?

"No," Jessica said. "He complains that we don't play it enough, and he feels as if it is now just a status symbol."

"Cool. Let's go play music." Clay felt for the door handle and headed through the door. By the time Jessica reached the piano, he was already sitting before it.

He inhaled. "I never get tired of feeling piano keys under my fingers." He played a chord and Jessica sat beside him, inhaling his scent and looking at his pensive expression as he effortlessly caressed the piano keys.

"When did you learn to play?" she asked softly.

"When I was seven," Clay said, "my mother sent me to classes. You know, I feel like playing the classics. Fur Elise comes to mind."

He started playing and Jessica closed her eyes. "This is good."

Clay then transitioned effortlessly into Pachelbel's Canon in D. Jessica joined him in the piece and they played together.

When the piece ended, Clay said softly. "Don't date

Khaled."

"Why?" Jessica whispered.

"There are so many reasons why you shouldn't," Clay said in the quietness of the living room, he could hear the old grandfather clock ticking. He was tempted to tell her what Khaled was really about, but he couldn't. He had to hope that she had the good sense to make the best choice for herself.

"Jessica," Clay gripped her hand. "Can you trust me on this?"

"I would if you told me why," Jessica said softly. "He seems to be a nice guy. He's genuine, sweet, and humble. I've been dreaming about this for years," she said to Clay, feeling that rush of surrealism that had overtaken her since she began tutoring Khaled.

"Tomorrow, I'll start giving him lessons."

"When?" Clay asked. His voice was husky.

"At seven, Mondays, and Wednesdays in Music Room 2. Why are you so against him?"

"I am not against him." Clay ran his fingers over the piano keys. "I just know him too well, that's all. Remember, I told you about Kara."

"Yes," Jessica said. "She called you at the airport and told you goodbye."

"Well, when we first met, I liked her. She was funny and warm, and I liked to hang out with her. I met her at a health food store. She was a health nut, and I was looking for a healthier way to live so we connected." He shrugged. "I liked her enough to introduce her to my uncle, and the guys at the studio. That was my first mistake. Khaled was there when the introductions were made.

She wanted to meet him so I casually introduced them. Next thing I knew she was sleeping with him. When I confronted her about it, she said she couldn't help it: he was her crush, her dream. Almost the same things you are saying to me now."

"But I won't..." Jessica started to protest.

"He is bad news," Clay said urgently. "Don't be blinded by his charm, okay. Keep your guard up." Clay moved close to Jessica on the chair. "Remember that you like me."

Jessica chuckled. "I do?"

"You know you do," Clay said softly. He was forehead to forehead with Jessica, their noses almost touching.

"I know it has been only three weeks, but we have something different. Something potent. Don't forget it, okay."

Jessica inhaled sharply. "I won't forget it, but Clay, it's Khaled. He's here... at Mount Faith. I don't know. I feel as if it's ordained, you know."

"But you like me, not him," Clay said softly. He kissed her and she opened her lips.

A clearing of the throat drew them apart. Jessica looked up and saw her father in his maroon red robe with the black sash, the one she and her siblings referred to as his world domination robe.

"Am I going to have to put you in a chastity belt?" he pointed to Jessica, "and you..." he glared at Clay, "tie a bell on you, so that I know what you are up to at night?"

He had a cup of tea in his hand and was watching the two of them quizzically.

"No, Sir," Clay said, happy that he couldn't see the scowl that he heard in Bancroft's voice.

"Well, good," Bancroft said. "I haven't heard good music in a while. I am going to sit over here. Play something Vivaldi."

Clay chuckled and Jessica rolled her eyes at her Dad who had made himself comfortable in one of the rocking chairs.

*****

Jessica entered Music Room 2 with a certain amount of trepidation, about three minutes before her class with Khaled was scheduled to start. Clay had warned her about him. Khaled was a player. She reiterated in her mind how much she liked Clay.

She really did. He was everything she liked in a guy. He played music, he wrote music, and he loved poetry. He was level-headed, serious, amazingly calm, rugged, and real. She was listing all his good qualities in her mind as she entered the music room, expecting to wait for Khaled, but she was surprised to see that he had showed up on time. He was sitting around the piano in his signature green and black color combo. She had expected that he would be fashionably late.

"Hi, Jessica," he looked sad. "I had a tough day."

"Really," Jessica asked, feeling a little thrill that Khaled was confiding in her. "How so?"

He flashed a smile at her. "There are so many fans up here. I can barely move around without a mob following in my wake."

Jessica smiled. "Yes, most of us have had Khaled fever at some points or the other."

Khaled sighed and sat down on the piano bench. "I just don't get it." His green eyes sparkled. "I thought it would have been refreshing to hear my real name, David Green, on the lips of people, but they all insist on calling me Khaled."

"I just wanted to be David for a while," he looked at Jessica. "The Khaled identity is like a mask. I want to remove it for a while and let people get to know the real me." He gripped his chest.

Jessica nodded. "I totally understand."

"I don't think you do, Jess," he said softly. "May I call you 'Jess'?"

"Yes," Jessica, said searching his eyes for any deception. All she saw was a tortured guy who was frustrated at losing his identity because he was a singer. He was not the monster that Clay was trying to portray to her, and so far he hadn't been self-centered either. He was an okay guy. She relaxed slightly.

"Well, Khaled, sorry, I mean David," she stuttered, trying hard to sound professional, "last class I realized that you have some rudimentary music skills. Teaching you shouldn't be too hard.

David nodded. "Yes. I am a quick learner." He turned to the piano and then turned back to look at her.

"Want to pick up dinner with me after this? I mean, I feel as if I can be ordinary around you. I am not asking you for a date. It's just that fame can make you so lonely and isolated, and you don't seem as star struck as everybody else around here."

"Well... er..." Jessica stuttered. "I am not..."

David smacked his head. "Oh, don't tell me you have a boyfriend."

"Well, I, er...not really," she said faintly. Technically, she and Clay were not officially together.

"You can ask him to come as well," David said, "that is, if he is as cool as you are. I wouldn't mind the extra company."

Jessica shook her head. If she told Clay, he would say 'no', and this was an opportunity to get to know Khaled/David better.

"Well, I'll be happy to come with you," she finally said after a small pause.

"Great." David nodded and flashed his dimpled smile at her again. "Let's get on with it, huh?"

David suggested that they go somewhere quiet after the piano lesson. "I hate to be interrupted when I am with someone as interesting as you." Jessica had literally blushed at that.

They ended up going to an off campus restaurant; it was a rustic place near the town square, that sold a decent curried goat.

"This is nice," David said, looking around at the sparse furnishings and the bare blue walls of the place. "It has the right amount of rugged."

Jessica smiled. "Yes, it does have that rustic feel to it, and the food is good too."

The owner came over to them, a white apron hanging askew around his neck. "What do you guys need?"

David said quickly, "I'll allow Jessica to order for me."

The owner grinned. "So then, that will be two curried goats and two small mannish water," he said, his hands akimbo. "Long time no see, Miss Jess."

Jessica grinned. "Yes, Mort, six long weeks."

He chuckled heartily and looked at David quizzically. "Is that all? We have desserts too, you know."

"No, that is all. Thanks," David said watching as the man walked off.

"I can't believe it," he said, looking at Jessica. "He didn't recognize me."

Jessica laughed. "Of course Mort recognizes you, but he is not star struck. Most of the people in these hills aren't. They couldn't care less about super stars."

A flash of anger crept over David's face, but he quickly hid it. "That's good. I mean this is the perfect place to have a vacation then."

Jessica nodded. "It could be."

"It's tranquil here. I would love to see more of the place

though. I mean, I just go to school and that's it."

He waited for Jessica to offer to take him exploring, but he realized that she was not as effusive as she should be and he wondered why. Maybe Clay had said something to her to poison her mind against him. He needed to work extra hard to gain her confidence now. He sighed inwardly. He wasn't used to working hard for any woman. This was going to be annoying.

Jessica was looking at Khaled and willing herself to feel the emotions she usually does when she hears his songs. She was feeling nothing, though he was handsome, and he was sitting right in front of her. This was her dream come true, but her treacherous heart wasn't budging. This situation felt too similar to the time when she assessed Ramon. No spark. No chemistry.

She was shaken out of her contemplation when Mort brought the food to their table.

"Tell me about Clay," she said to David, who was in the middle of talking about an Australia tour.

"Clay?" David frowned. "Clay Reid?" he asked again, as if he didn't hear. "What about him?"

"He really doesn't seem to...how should I put this...like you much," Jessica said. "I just want to understand where the animosity is coming from. Where did you guys meet?"

David shrugged. "At the studio. He works with Neil Reid. They call him a genius there because he comes up with original beats at the snap of a finger, and he writes some good songs as well. Everyone wants to work with Clay."

"I had no idea he was that good," Jessica said. "He doesn't really tell me anything about his musical life and he knows I am studying music," Jessica said. "I wonder why."

"He wants a break from all that, I guess." David worked hard to hide the petulance in his voice. Didn't this girl see how much better looking than Clay he was? He was the great Khaled. What was the matter with her? He turned the conversation around to himself.

"You know when my mother died and I left home, I had so many songs in my heart and I went to the iJam studios sad and broken."

Jessica's eyes softened in sympathy. "That must have been awful. That's why your first songs were filled with so much raw emotion."

David nodded. "Yes, they were. It was a rough time in my life, and the year after I got my heart broken quite unexpectedly."

"Why?" Jessica asked. "Why did she break up with you?"

"Because I was too busy touring and stuff. Back then the business had to come first." He wiped his mouth with a napkin and said to Jessica earnestly. "That's why I needed the break now so that I can really concentrate on a special person. You know, Jessica, I feel this connection between us. I remember when it came time for me to choose schools; I had this deep urge to come to Mount Faith. Now I'm thinking that it's because you are here."

Jessica gasped. "I've felt that way for years. Remember that song that you did: *I know you are out there, I am going to find where, and when I do, I'll know that you are the one.* I kinda thought you were talking about me."

David smiled slowly. "I wrote that song thinking that you were out there somewhere. Jessica, the girl in my dreams."

Jessica's heart lurched. This was it: her dream come true, and he had felt it too. Maybe her system was malfunctioning and she couldn't feel the connection between them just yet.

She tried to stifle the disquiet she was feeling and softly cursed Clay for putting so many doubts in her mind about Khaled. He was here. He was talking to her. He felt their connection.

He held her hand across the table. "I appreciate you being in my life now, Jessica." His eyes were so green that she could almost drown in their pure sincerity.

She waited for her pulse to quicken under his soft manicured fingers, but it didn't. Maybe it would take time. It was like an anticlimax. She had worked up herself to this moment, and when it actually happened it fell flat.

Chapter Eleven

The mid-October nights were reminding Clay that he was in a part of Jamaica that excelled in cool temperatures. He rubbed his hands together, hoping that the building's heater for their section of the library would kick in. He was in the science library with Ramon and four other group members working on their literature based group project. They had split up into twos to find specific topic areas to research. He was, of course, paired with Ramon.

His right eye was now completely clear. It had gradually come back, but it was still sensitive to light, and he had problems focusing on fine print. His left eye was still giving him grainy feedback, which was progress compared to the total blackness he was seeing before.

Most of the topics in the book he was staring at began to run into each other.

"Hey," Ramon said, carrying a big tome over to the table. "Found the book."

Clay nodded. "Where's the magnifying glass?"

"Beside you," Ramon said, and then he paused. "Did you know that Jess is secretly seeing Khaled?"

Clay nodded slowly. "I know. It's no secret. She announces it as soon as she gets in from work, or wherever. She usually looks at me defiantly when she says it, so I am taking a back seat to this."

"They are hanging out at Morts' restaurant every week. Khaled supposedly likes the quiet and he's calling her on the phone every other hour. It's sickening."

Ramon looked disturbed. "What are you doing about it? She's your girl. You live at her house. Shouldn't you be up in arms? Don't you want to just punch that stuck up punk in the mouth and tell him to leave Jess alone?"

Clay chuckled softly. "Calm down, Ramon. After she is exposed to him long enough, she will see that his feet are made of clay, and that he is just a man."

"But suppose he does something to her," Ramon asked. "You know, have sex with her or something. Suppose she falls in love with him."

Clay clenched his fist. "Then she'd be stupid. I warned her about him already. Jessica is twenty-one; she is a woman. She has to make up her mind about Khaled without any interference from me, or I guess she'll always wonder what would've happened if she had given him a chance. She has to get him out of her system. I know him; his true colors will soon start showing."

Ramon gritted his teeth. "I can't stand him. There is something about him that makes me want to snarl."

Clay chuckled. "He is too smooth, too charming?"

"Yes, that's it." Ramon clicked his fingers. "And he sails around campus expecting everyone to worship him. It's disturbing. You know, I even see the older administrators giggling and talking to him like they have lost their senses."

Clay nodded. "He loves that kind of thing."

"So why did he retire then?" Ramon asked, puzzled. "If adoration is like air to him, why is he up here? Shouldn't he be singing at some sold out concert halfway across the globe?"

Clay tapped the table uneasily. "Look Ramon. I think this is just what Khaled wants, us to be saying about him. Let's forget him for the time being and get on with this project."

Ramon nodded, but he was still uneasy with the whole Khaled issue. He looked at Clay contemplatively; he did not know Jessica for as long as he did. He wouldn't know how severely attached to Khaled she was, or how much she had personally invested in him. He could not allow Khaled to hurt her. He was going to spend all his spare time watching him.

*****

Ramon Rodriguez, detective. Ramon felt like saying drolly to the security at the gate when he drove in. He had been following Khaled for the past nine days, and understood why Clay was not so concerned about Jessica being too into Khaled. He saw the two of them interacting on Wednesday in front of the Music Building, and he could safely say that Jessica wasn't looking as if she was hero worshipping as he thought she would be. She held her body away from his, she laughed shrilly and insincerely at his jokes, and she was not talking as animatedly as he knew she did when she really liked someone.

They stood in front of the building and spoke for ten minutes, and then she got into her car. She looked pensive, not at all relaxed, nor happy, not like the way she looked with Clay. He smiled to himself when he saw that. He could breathe a sigh of relief, but he would still monitor that situation to see how it was going.

He followed Khaled to Blue Palm Apartment after that and was about to give up his detective work for the night because he had a meeting with his project group in a short while. Instead, his interest was peaked when he was about to reverse out of the parking lot and saw Khaled stop to talk with a guy who was wearing a black hat and had his hands in his pockets. He stopped the car and craned his neck, trying to see who it could be. The body language of the guy looked very familiar. Just then, another car drove into the parking and its headlights illuminated the guys face. He saw that it was Stewart.

Stewart Rhoden, the guy who had accidentally lit the gun powder when Clay was looking through the microscope. He was talking animatedly to Khaled, and when the car lights went off, Ramon actually saw them hug. It was a reassuring tap on the back, the kind of thumping hug and pat on the back that only friends do with each other. Ramon started the car and drove out of the parking lot. That was puzzling and very strange. He didn't know those two were friends.

*****

"I wish Khaled would do a concert up here," a girl sitting to the left of him in the library was whispering fiercely to her friends.

"I wish the president hadn't sent us the advisory that if we hounded David Khaled Green in anyway while he was on the Mount Faith campus we would be suspended. What kind of notice is that? does he think we are groupies?"

"I got a picture with him," her perky friend said. "Here it

is on my phone."

They both looked over it and squealed. "I love him. I want to have his babies."

Her other friend laughed. "In your dreams. I heard he is dating Jessica Bancroft."

Clay looked around at the two of them angrily. "Are you girls aware that this is a library?"

"Geesh." They looked across at him in disgust. "We are discussing current affairs."

Clay got his books together and his trusty magnifying glass and moved deeper into the science section. He considered checking out the book and reading it at home, but it wasn't on the list of books that could be taken from the library. He had to finish his assigned task because he was determined that he would not be the weak link in the group project.

He was perusing the book when a paper was slapped down on top of it.

He looked up. It was Khaled.

"That," Khaled said, "is a come out of retirement Khaled petition signed by three hundred students in the last day and a half."

"Well, do it. Continue," Clay said exasperatedly. He pushed the paper off and went back to his book.

"What did you say to Jessica?" Khaled growled. "She is treating me like I have a contagious disease."

Clay chuckled. "Good girl."

Khaled sat down across from him and folded his arms. "I bet you warned her that I was a player and that I was only after one thing."

Clay shrugged. "Or maybe she just doesn't like you. Maybe she can smell phony from a mile off."

"Well I have a plan for your precious Jessica," Khaled said. "I am going to see if she doesn't thaw toward me when

I lay it on her. You know, the thing is Jessica is hard to read, but I think I have discovered her kryptonite."

Clay looked up from the textbook. "Leave me alone David...Khaled...whatever you are calling yourself. Go and rack up some more petitions to soothe your over inflated ego."

Khaled got up and growled. "I hate it when you put on that smug look. Let's see if you are still so smug after I'm finished with your girlfriend."

Chapter Twelve

Digital Broadcast Media was Jessica's only night class. Usually it would fascinate her, but for the past few weeks she had been going through a metamorphosis. She was confused and feeling lack luster and quite unlike her self. She waited impatiently for the class to end. Clay had declared tonight movie night in celebration of him being able to see clearly from his right eye; he was also inviting over Ramon.

She knocked the pen on the desk. She was looking forward to movie night more than she was to seeing Khaled. She was even mixing up his name in her head. It was nothing like what she thought it would be. He was clearly interested in her, but her long held crush was gone.

She was trying to hang onto the feeling for dear life, trying to recapture how she felt in the past, but the excitement and the chemical imbalance that was supposed to allow her to act like a maniac had drained away. She only felt that way about Clay these days. Why did Clay have to come to Mount Faith when he did? He was destroying all her long held fantasies in one swoop.

She actually woke up looking forward to seeing him at the breakfast table in the mornings, and she went to bed with a smile on her face knowing that he was just down the hall. She was also listening to Khaled's songs differently. In the past, she would imagine him running his fingers along the piano, especially as he did the soulful solo pieces. Now, that glorious vision was ruined because she knew that Khaled couldn't even play the piano, and she had a feeling that he was not interested in learning how to. Her fantasies were crumbling, one by one.

She didn't realize that class was over. Students were still seated, but the lecturer had turned off her mike and was answering questions from some students at the front. A voice said behind her.

"Delivery for Miss Jessica Bancroft." When she looked around, there was a guy with a big bouquet of blood red roses. Other persons were also looking over at her. She sank lower in the seat. She disliked being the center of attention like this.

"Yes," she said weakly.

"Please sign here." He shoved a paper at her and placed the flowers on the desk.

"From Khaled," the guy said loudly. "He says 'if you were mine I'd give you the world.'"

Jessica shrunk even further into her seat. Some people were clapping and saying, "Aww."

The guy moved away, and she looked at the perfumed flowers. There looked to be about three-dozen of them in an expensive glazed clay jar.

Clay, she thought, as she inhaled the pungent aroma from the flowers. She just got a grand gesture from Khaled, and she was thinking about Clay. She almost jumped when a hand landed on her shoulder.

"Sorry to startle you." Vanley walked around to her line of vision and sat beside her.

She grinned in relief at her cousin. "What are you doing here?"

"Chauffer services. Davia is working late. I was in the building, and I curiously followed the guy with the flowers. He created quite a stir in the lobby. All the ladies were swooning behind him. What is it about women and flowers? I sent a bouquet to Davia once, and she still talks about it as if it's a big deal."

"It's a big deal for some women," Jessica said. "It's not my thing though and if the sender knew me, he'd know that. I find this super corny. It's just not me."

Vanley sat in the seat beside her and then looked at the note. 'If you were mine, I'd give you the world? Khaled.'

"Yup," Jessica said, turning off her laptop.

"You don't look overwhelmed by the gesture, and we all know how much you love Khaled." Vanley said, frowning. "Are you okay, Jess?"

"I am feeling out of sorts," Jessica said softly. People were slowly filing past her seat and stopping to admire the flowers. "And I don't love Khaled."

So she finally admitted it aloud. It was such a relief when she said it, like she had gotten an epiphany. It was a defining moment for her; she needed to examine that statement when she was alone in her bed tonight.

She almost missed Vanley's murmured reply.

"Run that by me again?" She asked Vanley when she realized that she was looking at him and wasn't hearing a word.

"I said, that statement sounds a bit like the situation when the devil carried Jesus on a high mountain and showed him all the kingdoms of the world and their glory and said, 'All these will I give you, if you fall down and worship me.'"

Jessica shook her head. "It's not the same thing."

Vanley grinned. "Probably not. You have willingly worshipped Khaled for years, so this invitation is moot."

"No," Jessica said uncomfortably. "What is worship?"

"To show reverence and adoration for someone—to God, worship is a big deal."

Jessica felt uncomfortable. "I might have gone overboard with my... er... adoration of Khaled, but that was before I met him." She looked at Vanley troubled. "Reality is catching up with me."

Vanley squeezed her shoulder. "I am not judging you."

"I know," Jessica said. "Actually, that's the reason I am not too happy. I just don't feel it, you know, and I'm not sure why. I was so into him, and now he is here in the flesh, yet I'm not feeling it anymore."

"The scales have fallen from your eyes," Vanley said ruefully.

"Yes, I guess," Jessica said. "I must be coming down with something."

Vanley shook his head. "No you are not. I can confidently say that because I was in a somewhat similar situation couple months ago."

Jessica pushed the laptop in the bag and got up. "With Anita?"

Vanley nodded. "With Anita. Reality is a tough lady to deal with, huh?"

"Talk to you later?" She picked up the flowers and sneezed.

"Sure," Vanley responded.

*****

When Jessica walked into the house with the flowers in hand, Ramon and Clay were already in the living room.

"Hey Jess," Ramon said, "Clay chose a chick flick just because you'd like it."

Jessica put down the flowers, and Clay and Ramon looked at it and then at her.

"A chick flick," she said heading over to the settee and sitting between the two of them. "That sounds like fun."

"Er...aren't we going to talk about the 'perfumy' bundle of bush in the corner?" Ramon asked, raising his eyebrows at Jessica.

"No," Jessica said. She shifted closer to Clay and put her head on his shoulder. "I just want to watch the chick flick."

Ramon shook his head and raised his eyebrows at Clay.

Clay ignored his prodding to say something and put an arm around Jessica instead.

"She gets flowers but she comes home to me."

Ramon chuckled. "Well...you do have a point."

When the movie was half way through, Clay quietly asked Jessica, "Doesn't he know that you hate roses?"

"Nope," Jessica said. "When we talk, he constantly talks about himself: where he went to do a concert, who he met, who knows him, who likes him, how crappy his life was before fame, how happy he is now. He is annoying."

Ramon turned down the television and laughed. "I live to hear this. Did Jessica say that Khaled is annoying?"

"Might as well you pause the show," Clay said to Ramon. "You seem to be getting very sleepy."

Ramon pressed the pause button on the remote in relief.

Jessica, who still had her head on Clay's chest said softly, "So it's movie night but Ramon is sleepy, Clay is not really watching, and I'm thinking."

"Yes," Ramon said, "it's those flowers. They smell too sweet. They are putting me to bed. Maybe the florist sprayed them with perfume to enhance the scent. It's stifling. I can't recall them smelling like that in nature."

Jessica raised her head up from Clay's chest. "You really dislike Khaled, don't you?"

"Yes," Ramon said. "And I have been spying on him these past couple of days, and from what I can see the only class he's attending is yours." He looked at Clay. "I don't want to start anything, but he hangs out with Stewart a lot, mostly at Blue Palm Apartments."

Clay inhaled. "Are you sure?"

"Yup," Ramon said, "I find it odd that he is hanging with the guy who lit the gunpowder that almost blinded you."

Clays lips twisted. "It must be coincidence," he said aloud, but he wasn't really thinking that. It all made sense to him now.

Jessica said, disgruntled. "You guys don't mind if I retire early. I really feel weird, you know, like you would before a flu."

"Okay," Clay kissed her on her forehead.

When she left Ramon got up too. "I am going to leave as well, Clay."

"Hey man, thanks for spying on Khaled."

"No problem," Ramon said. He headed to the door and sniffed a flower from the bouquet. "Smells as fake as the sender."

When he left Clay turned off the television and sat alone in the dark, thinking.

Chapter Thirteen

David 'Khaled' Green had done many things in his life, but stealing was not one of them. He needed somebody to break into Clay's apartment. He needed that book of poetry that Clay always lugged around. He was near desperate to get the attention and the affection of Jessica Bancroft and he had belatedly realized that the usual gestures were not going to work. He was even seeing signs of contempt and distrust in her eyes.

What was Clay telling that girl about him? She was slowly but surely withdrawing herself from him and warming up to Clay, who was blind, and to him, merely a student. She had gotten her priorities twisted, and he had to remind her that he was the one she had a crush on for years.

That's why he needed Clay's poetry book. Jessica loved poetry and poetic things; Clay was the same. Clay was a poetic person at heart. Neil Reid would say that he was an old soul. He always wrote down his thoughts in a big book, and those thoughts usually found their way into songs. He was sure that Clay must have some new material in that book.

Khaled snorted. Neil Reid only cared for two things: his profit margin and Clay. He couldn't stand the two of them, but he needed them and it irked him. He stubbed his toe on a side table and cursed fluently. Everything was conspiring against him, even the cheap-looking table.

He needed that book of poems; he needed Jessica Bancroft to like him. He would prefer if she fell in love with him because he could see that she was Clay's weakness. He wanted to hurt Clay, but not only that, he would have something with which to bargain with Clay since he cared so much about Jessica.

That girl was stronger and more self-possessed than she looked; added to that, she had a big bad family in her back pocket. He would have to tread softly, real softly where she was concerned.

He needed that book. That book was the kryptonite. That would have Jessica's poetry-loving heart beating for him. The knock on his door couldn't have come soon enough for him. When he peeped through the keyhole, he saw that it was Stewart.

He opened the door and dragged him in. "Why did you take so long to get here?" he hissed to his friend.

"I had to be careful that no one saw me." Stewart hissed back, shrugging off his hand when he got into the room. "So what's the deal? Why did you drag me from my domino game in the student lounge?"

"I need you to break into Clay's apartment next door," Khaled said, "I need his poetry book. Don't ransack the place I need it to be as neat as possible. I don't want any trouble, and don't want anyone suspecting me."

Stewart shook his head. "I would have to wait until the

block is completely still, that would be around three o'clock. The locks around here are easy to pick. I have gone into Tracy's apartment several times without her knowing."

David snorted. "When I said you should pretend to be that girl's boyfriend I only asked because she was in the apartment beside Clay's."

Stewart nodded. "I know. I liked her a lot though. At least she responded to me like duck to water, unlike how Jessica Bancroft is responding to you. I thought you said that this would have been a foolproof plan?"

"It was supposed to be, but that girl is a hard nut to crack. She's a true creative, cerebral type. Nothing seems to be working with her. I send her flowers; I tell her how famous I am, trying to impress her, and she withdraws." Khaled sat in one of the uncomfortable chairs and crossed his legs. "I can't stand this place. It is so primitive."

Stewart chuckled. "Unfortunately, universities do not cater to pop stars; they cater to ordinary students."

"It's been three weeks now." Khaled growled. "Why isn't that girl into me yet?"

"Because for once, a girl just prefers Clay to David."

"I look better, I dress better, and I am famous." He threw up his hand in the air. "What's the deal?"

"Maybe she likes Clay because she can sense that he genuinely likes her. You know children and animals respond to inner kindness."

David growled. "What do you know?

"Clay is a genuinely nice guy and you are not. There is a cold edge to you."

"Remember who is paying you," David said sternly, "and whose friend you are."

"I remember," Stewart said, "and thanks for thinking of me for this gig. It is the most profitable gig I've had all year, and even though I am no actor, I pulled off that stunt in the lab really well."

"Shut up," David said. He was feeling a bit paranoid about what he asked Stewart to do to Clay. Even for him, that was pushing the boundaries too far. "Suppose somebody is listening?"

Stewart sat down across from him. "Nobody suspects me as being anything else other than what I am, a regular student. Who would be listening? David, this jealousy of Clay is getting to your head. At the risk of me losing some money, I need to know why you are so interested in him. Can't you get another songwriter and producer? After all, you are Khaled. You are the talent. Clay is just one of many service people."

David shook his head. "He is a genius. You don't understand. Everything he touches in the studio comes to life. My career would not be the same without him."

"That's why he leaves and then you announce your retirement?"

"Something like that," Khaled said. "Without him, my career is as good as dead."

"You could go out and forge your own destiny," Stewart said. "You are well known; you can write your ticket for any other studio. You don't need iJam."

David shook his head. "But I do. More than you know. Just get me that book of poems."

When Stewart got the book of poems in the wee hours of the morning, David almost salivated at the wealth of material in it. The first one was Golden Girl, where Clay described Jessica. He loved it. It would make a great song.

He grabbed his phone. There was no time like the present to start wooing Jessica Bancroft. He would do it properly this time, the way that she wanted it. He was now playing on her terms. He sent her the first verse of the poem via text message and lay down in his student's bed with a smile on his face. Let's see if she can resist that. He almost laughed at his cunning maneuver.

*****

When the sun touches her hair, it's like golden sparks, the type of gold that sparkles like good wine that never goes flat.

Jessica read the text several times for the day and found herself smiling each time. He really can write. She was feeling the attraction for Khaled that she thought had been lost come roaring back.

She wasn't surprised when she saw him outside her last class with his hand in his pocket, standing beside a champagne colored Range Rover.

He waved to her, and when she came near he said softly, "And when she smiles, my heart quickens in reply, thundering in my ear. She is poetry in motion."

Jessica's smile got even wider. "Hey."

"Hey," David said softly. "I was wondering if you got my text."

"I did." Jessica nodded. "It's really pretty. I like it."

"And I like you," David said easily. "What are you up to this evening?"

"Nothing much," Jessica said slowly. "I have a poetry society meeting. Want to come with me?"

"You guys have that here? I would really love to come; I do love poetry."

Jessica looked at him, pleased. "You know, this is exactly how I imagined it would go when you first came here."

"It was?" David smiled slowly.

"Yeah," Jessica nodded. "I am just now seeing the artist

in you."

David mused. "I was trying to hold it down, you know… didn't want to seem as if I was a show off or anything."

"I would not have thought that at all," Jessica said. "I really love the words of your songs and I…," she bent her head shyly, "I know they had to come from a heart that felt deeply, and I am just happy that I am seeing this side of you."

David touched her hair. "I am sorry I never showed it before."

Jessica smiled at him warmly. "Want to go to the Business Center for something to eat before the meeting?"

"Sure," David said, "and then you can tell me all about you. I just realize that I don't know anything much about you."

*****

On the last day of October, Clay realized two things as he was sitting around the Bancroft's breakfast table. Firstly, Jessica was not making eye contact with him anymore, and secondly, he could see out of his left eye much better. He could move out now, back to Blue Palm Apartments without having any issues.

He set his glasses firmer on his nose bridge. He couldn't do that, not when Jessica was suddenly being secretive, not when he suspected that her feelings for Khaled had changed.

What could have caused this sudden warming to Khaled?

He watched her as she sneaked a look on her phone screen. Another text. He saw her eyes light up.

He wanted to ask her what it said. He was glad when a grumpy looking Dr. Bancroft did it for him.

"What's so funny, Jessica?"

Jessica cleared her throat and looked at all of them

sheepishly. "Nothing."

Bancroft grunted.

Clay wanted to shake her. It seemed as if she had buried everything that he had told her about Khaled and was giving him a chance. Khaled had figured out that flowers were not going to work, so obviously he had been trying a new approach. What had he called it, her kryptonite? What was Jessica's kryptonite?

He heard the ping on her phone indicating that another text was received, and then he got it. The old schemer was using poetry. But Khaled didn't know any poetry. He was not very poetic. The extent of his repertoire was 'roses are red, violets are blue'.

Throughout breakfast he watched Jessica closely, and when she was finished he hurriedly got up as well. "Hey, Jess, want me to walk you to class?"

Jessica looked at him, a little guilt in her glance. "Sure."

"What's wrong?" Clay asked when they were on their way down the driveway. Dr. Bancroft's dog, Daryl, was loping beside them, but he stopped before they could open the gate.

Jessica looked at the dog and said, "Bye, Daryl," before she closed the gate.

Clay could see that she didn't want to answer the question. She had secrets, and he was sure that they involved Khaled, and he was sure that he was not going to like what he heard. He felt a tight hold of jealousy gripping him, and she had not even spoken yet.

"I like Khaled, I mean David again," Jessica finally said. "You and I have not really been official and so...," she shrugged, "I didn't see a need to tell you."

Clay inhaled. The cool morning air tangled with his lungs, almost burning him as he held on to it before he finally exhaled. The burning sensation was still there. He wanted to shout at her, shake her. What did she mean she didn't see a need to tell him?

He wanted to tell her how deceitful David was, but he knew he couldn't say anything without telling her the whole story, and he couldn't tell her the whole story because he was heavily involved in it. He bit his lip and grunted.

Jessica glanced at him. "I am sorry, okay, but you and I were just..."

"We could have been really good together," Clay said hoarsely, before she could give him her Dear John speech in favor of her precious Khaled. He didn't want to hear it. He walked faster which had her fighting to catch up. He almost laughed bitterly at the irony of it. Usually it was the other way around, but anger was propelling him faster than anything else could.

"Wait, Clay," Jessica said, "I am just hanging out with him. It's not serious."

Clay sighed and looked behind at her. "You are playing with fire, Jess."

Jessica slowed down and watched him walk away. Who was fire, Clay, or Khaled? She really wished that she weren't so caught up with the two of them. Her simple life was now getting so complicated.

Chapter Fourteen

Clay called his uncle as soon as he reached the science building and enclosed himself in an alcove where he knew nobody could hear him. He was breathing hard; he wasn't sure if it was the walk or the anger that had him so worked up.

He felt jittery. He jabbed the numbers on his phone and paced while he waited for his uncle to answer. When he finally did, he realized that his voice was quivery.

"Listen uncle, I want to know what's the connection between Stewart Rhoden and David Green?"

"Ah," Neil said, "you have finally come to the realization that that boy being at Mount Faith was a well-orchestrated move."

"Yes," Clay hissed, "and that my almost being blinded was no coincidence."

"How is the eye?" Neil asked breezily. He had long come to that conclusion so he was not as agitated as Clay.

"My eyes are almost fine. The left one is coming back. The doctor said they will be back to normal in a few weeks."

"When are you coming back home?" his uncle said after a pause.

Clay felt trapped. His independence was very much at stake here. He hated this feeling of not being able to do what he wanted, but with David at Mount Faith trying to woo Jessica, and on the verge of succeeding, he didn't know what to do. He could have easily taken anything that David had coming his way but he didn't want Jessica to get hurt.

He sighed. "I don't want to come back to the studio just now," he said faintly.

"Just do one more album," Neil said softly, "and the contract will be fulfilled. I promise you that I will leave you alone to do whatever you want to do with your future. At the very least, if you do this it will get David off your back."

Clay grunted. "I don't know..."

"How many courses do you have left?" Neil asked, smelling capitulation.

"Two, next semester," Clay said, "and then I am done."

"Do you have to do them there?" Neil asked. "Why don't you do them while we work on the seventh album? I promise I won't put any pressure on you."

Clay hung his head and stared at the tip of his sneakers. If he agreed to his uncle's offer, he would be telling Jessica goodbye in December. Maybe she wouldn't miss him anyway. The thought made him grit his teeth.

"Okay," he said to his uncle. "I'll do it."

Neil whooped. "Yes!"

Clay hung up the phone and felt a light feeling take him over.

"Hey, what's wrong?"

He looked up reluctantly and saw that the person asking

him was Stewart. He grimaced. "How much is David paying you to follow me?"

Stewart frowned and came nearer to him. "What are you talking about, Clay?"

"You've been pretty scarce around here since you blinded me," Clay said, "but then again, I couldn't see so I wouldn't know, would I?"

He didn't even feel angry toward Stewart. He felt like shaking David Green, the self-centered prig, right this minute.

Stewart frowned. "I don't know what are you talking about."

Clay sighed. "I know okay. I can see fairly well again, and I put two and two together."

"I knew your eye wouldn't be permanently blinded," Stewart said smugly. "The same thing happened to me when I was younger, and I had no ill effects. You see I know a thing or two about chemistry, and David said he wanted you temporarily incapacitated. That experiment was a God send."

Clay snorted." Excuse me if I don't have the same reaction. Did you come up here to Mount Faith just to spy on me?"

Stewart sat across from him. "Yup. I enrolled shortly after you did."

"And all of that madness about Tracy was fake, wasn't it?"

"Yup," Stewart said unrepentantly. "I made it up to have a story. I dated her just in case. Let me tell you, that girl is a handful. It was the longest two months of my life."

"Was she really seeing Ray?" Clay asked curiously.

Stewart nodded. "Apparently she was using him to build some super secret perfume thing for some class or the other she was taking. He did it, and now they have parted ways."

Clay sighed. "I should have you and David locked up for

assault or conspiracy to do bodily harm. That carries some jail time, doesn't it?"

Stewart looked at him. "Yes, it does. That's the reaction I expected when you were first blinded, but what I found intriguing was that David told me that you wouldn't do that. He said that you didn't want any publicity. What's the deal with you, David, and your uncle?"

"David isn't much of a friend if he hasn't told you everything," Clay said wearily.

"I guess. If I were more curious, I would figure it out myself," Stewart said, shrugging.

Clay sighed. "I have a class. Unlike you, I really came up here to finish a degree."

Stewart stood up and watched him as he walked away. He was glad that he didn't have to pretend to go to the classes anymore because he sensed that his time at Mount Faith was coming to an end.

*****

It was raining when Khaled called Jessica. "Want to go for an evening stroll?"

Jessica looked across at Clay. He was sitting in the living room in the chair across from her. He had his big science book open and was perusing it with a magnifying glass.

After their conversation this morning, she had kind of expected that he would move out. She knew that he could now see properly from both eyes. She dreaded coming home, thinking that he was not going to be around.

Her heart still did that weird thing when she saw him, but she suppressed it. He was just a guy. She was getting to know the real Khaled, the one she had always wanted. There could be no space for Clay.

"Or," Khaled was saying in her ear, "you could come and help me to finish this poem that I started. I entitled it, *Jessica*."

Jessica laughed uncomfortably, glancing at Clay. "You did?"

"Yes." Khaled breathed in her ear. "If you asked me the question who is she, the answer would be that Jessica is the girl for me."

"Khaled," Jessica said breathlessly, "that's so sweet." She got up because Clay had looked up when she said "Khaled", and his eyes were eating her alive. She could actually feel the heat from them.

She moved toward her room. "I can't leave my house; it is raining cats and dogs."

"I am outside," Khaled said, "and it's not that bad. I can make a mean hot chocolate at my apartment to chase away the chills."

Jessica glanced at Clay who had swiveled around to watch her progress, and then she said breathlessly. "Okay, I'll be right there."

"Stop looking at me like that," she said when she hung up the phone.

Clay grimaced. "Sorry. It's a privilege to see you. After the accident I vowed to take advantage of sight for as long as I can."

"I am going out," Jessica said defiantly.

She went into her room and grabbed her raincoat, completely missing Clay's crumpling expression.

When she got up, he had schooled his face into a calm he did not feel. "I'll wait up."

"Don't wait up. I am an adult; I know what I am doing. Leave me alone."

She already felt bad and guilty, and she didn't want him to

sit there with his long-suffering martyr expression and judge her. She had waited her whole life for Khaled. She didn't want anybody to rain on her parade.

She opened the front door. The visibility was poor. There was even a fog over the hills in the distance. She walked down to Khaled's car; inside was mercifully warm.

"Hey," she said.

"Hey." He was in a red shirt; his dimples showed as he flashed a smile at her. He was gorgeous. Her wayward heart, which once had only shown signs of movement for Clay, was now fully functional, and it was racing a mile a minute for Khaled.

He smelled good. He leaned over her to check if she had her seat belt on right and brushed her breasts in the process.

He smiled at her warmly. "I know this must sound weird," he said softly, "but I love weather like this."

"Me too," Jessica said. "I had this fantasy once…" She shook her head. She shouldn't tell him about her fantasy of both of them kissing with the elements crashing around them.

"What, Jessica?" he asked, his green eyes lighting up.

"Nothing. I might tell you another day." She looked back at the house; the curtains had shifted, and Clay's silhouette was at the window.

"Lets get out of here," she said hurriedly.

David chuckled. "Is he seeing better now?"

"Yes. Sort of."

"So why don't you kick him out? David asked. "Hasn't he overstayed his welcome?"

Jessica swallowed. She didn't want to talk about Clay and she didn't want to kick him out, as David had so casually put it.

"He's okay," Jessica said lamely. What she felt for Clay

couldn't be put into words. Mixed up was more like it. One thing was for sure: a part of her wanted him near.

*****

When Jessica let herself inside later that night, she glanced at her watch; it was twenty minutes after twelve. She had really had a good time. She had sat with Khaled and listened to music. He told her what inspired some of her favorite songs, and they talked about everything and nothing. It had been cozy and intimate and such a great time that she didn't wanted to leave.

She glanced at the settee. True to his word Clay was up. He looked at her as she opened the door and then back into his book.

"Goodnight," she said defiantly.

He didn't answer. Jessica's previous high suddenly deflated. He was making her feel really bad, like she was a cheater or something. She walked off to her room, looking at the back of his head before she closed her door and leaned on it. She was torturing herself with Clay around; she should ask him to leave.

Clay stopped pretending that he was reading his textbook and closed it when he heard the click of her door. He closed his eyes rubbing them tiredly.

"Enlighten me." He jumped when he heard the gruff voice behind him. Bancroft walked into his line of vision and sat down in his favorite rocking chair.

"About what?" Clay asked curiously.

Bancroft looked at him his eyebrow raised. "Your sight is back?"

Clay nodded.

"And you are still here," Bancroft frowned, "while my

daughter is seeing that singer."

Clay shrugged. "Sorry, Dr. Bancroft; I can always leave."

"No," Bancroft shook his head. "I don't want you to leave. You can stay here. I find this fascinating. How do you feel about Jessica?"

"I..." Clay sighed, "I...like her a lot."

Bancroft nodded. "So why are you passively waiting while she goes out with this Khaled guy."

Clay shook his head and looked down at his fingers. "I am not passive Sir. I am pathetic."

"Explain," Bancroft said, looking at him contemplatively, like he was a puzzle that he had yet to solve.

"If I leave Mount Faith," he inhaled and then exhaled rapidly, "it will solve everything. The truth is…" He paused. He couldn't really say what the truth was, could he? A half-truth would be better. "I am the reason that Khaled is pursuing Jessica. If I leave, he leaves with me."

"Why?" Bancroft asked.

Clay looked at the president of the school in his maroon colored robe and his matching slippers. He shouldn't look so commanding, but he did, and though he would dearly love to confide in him, he couldn't.

"He followed me here," Clay said. The grandfather clock's loud ticking in the dining room could be heard in the silence.

Bancroft frowned. "I don't like secrets. I am tired of them. Every single one of my children has been tainted by some mystery or secret surrounding their relationship. I was hoping that Jessica would be different."

Clay nodded.

"Whatever it is that you are doing, Clay Reid, don't you dare let that Khaled guy hurt her."

Clay nodded contemplatively, "I won't."

"Because if he does," Bancroft said, "I am blaming you."

Clay nodded again and then glanced at the piano. "It won't wake up Mrs. B if I play?"

Bancroft shook his head. "No, go ahead. She wasn't sleeping; Jessica was out. Don't think that you were the only one up."

Clay got around the piano and played "Find You", one of his favorite songs from Khaled's third album. *If I knew who you were, I would have found you a long time ago.*

When he finished playing the notes, Bancroft looked at him speculatively and got up. He was shaking his head and then he left the living room.

Jessica heard the haunting tune from her room and almost got up to join him. He played it exactly the way that Khaled did. Well, not Khaled, he couldn't play. He played it the same way that it was played on the album.

Chapter Fifteen

Clay was on count down. It was the start of December. He had just three weeks left before exams. He could finish the last three credits he had to do next year with the Mount Faith branch in Kingston.

He had had the crappiest few weeks. David had stepped up his game with Jessica, and Clay had the unenviable experience of seeing the girl he loved fall under the spell of a guy who was not genuine in the least, but he couldn't say a thing.

He still lived in her house though. She had not once suggested that he leave, and her parents seemed quite fine with him there. He stood in the middle of the courtyard at the Business Center, waiting for Ramon; they had a bunch of things to do to finish the project before exams. After that, he could take a breather. He was fast realizing that school and romance were hard to deal with together.

"Hey, man," Adrian Bancroft almost walked past him in

the Business Center. He was with his little daughter. They had often visited the house, and he had gotten to know them somewhat, especially the friendly little girl, Avia. She looked so much like a miniature Jessica, with her brown hair and matching brown eyes.

He waved to Adrian and watched as Avia's eyes lit up when she saw him. That was how Jessica's eyes used to light up when she saw him, but these days he was lucky if she gave him a long glance. She was doing a good enough job of pretending that he was not around.

"Hi," Avia waved at him. She had recently lost a tooth, and her endearing gap-toothed smile made him smile as well.

"Hi." He watched as they walked toward the cafeteria and then he decided to take a seat. He was just standing in the middle of the walkway like a lost soul. Eventually, he sat down near the entrance to the Center, near a patch of sun and put his rucksack on the table. He needed to review the papers for the project.

"So you are seeing well enough now, Stevie Wonder?" David's snarky voice asked him.

Clay looked up, squinting a bit. "Yes, no thanks to you. Suppose Stewart had blinded me with that little stunt?"

David sat down. "Keep your voice down."

Clay looked at him balefully. "What's the matter, came to gloat about Jessica?"

David grinned. "She is a really tough lady to bed. Can I tell you how tired I am getting of her and her poetry? I mean I stayed up all night last week Thursday trying to swot Rudyard Kipling's 'If' just to impress her. I feel as if I am in school. Why did you have to choose this kind of girl to like? Kara was so much easier."

Clay resisted the urge to react.

"I tell you though," David said, rubbing his hands together.

"Tonight is the night."

Clay tapped his fingers on the table; he wanted to ring David's neck. "I am going back to Kingston as soon as this semester is over. I'll do the seventh album."

David nodded. "Neil told me, but I..." he scratched his chin, "I have this urge to conquer Jessica. She's the toughest challenge I have ever had to endure."

Clay got up.

"No wait, sit down," David said, an evil grin on his lips. "I promise. When I finally conquer Jessica, I will not tell you the details like I told you about Kara. I swear."

Clay pushed the papers he had just taken out back into his rucksack; this was all his fault. He should have packed up and left Mount Faith a long time ago.

"She's your Achilles heel," David said, almost salivating, "and I can't resist."

He laughed an evil laugh that had Clay gritting his teeth. "I can't wait to be rid of you," he said, keeping his voice low, "and when I do, it will be a wonderful day for me."

David sobered up. "You shouldn't be complaining, Clay. Things have always been easy for you. You have a nice family—a mother who cares, and a father and uncle who are protective of you—and you have great musical talent. What do I have? Nothing much really, when you think of it. You and your sniveling uncle owe me, and don't you two forget it."

"I owe you nothing," Clay said. "There was a time, a long time ago, when I thought I did, but guess what? I was nearly the same age as you when you walked into our lives, and I became the one who had to sacrifice all my dreams for your ambitions. This is the very last time," Clay said savagely, "and then I want you to leave me alone. Got that! You are toxic. You complain and bellyache over the same thing over and over again. It stops here."

David swallowed. He saw the determined look in Clay's eyes, and suddenly he wished that Clay were still wearing those dark glasses. All the contempt that he had bottled up inside was plain to see.

*****

When Clay reached home in the evening, he was not in the mood for conversation. He saw Celeste in the living room. She was holding her newest grandbaby. Kylie had given birth a few short weeks before to a little boy who looked very much like his father. Kylie was visiting. He could hear her voice in the direction of Jessica's room.

She walked into the hallway and smiled at him. "Hey, Clay."

He nodded to her and saw that Jessica was behind her. She was in a tight red dress and black boots. She looked all dolled up to go out with David, who was bent on seduction tonight. He felt his ears heating up. How could Jessica be so foolish? Couldn't she see through that wolf in sheep's clothing yet?

For weeks, he had been giving her space to see the deception for herself. He expected that she would have come to her senses by now, but here she was, looking like a million dollars and wasting her emotions on a man who wanted to use and discard her just to spite him. He stood where he was in the hallway. Kylie gave him a puzzled smile.

Jessica started to edge pass him and gave him that stealthy, guilty look that she had been giving him for the past couple of weeks. He held out his hand and stopped her. She widened her eyes and looked at him as if she were frightened. What did she have to be afraid of? Her mother was a few feet behind them in the living room, and her sister had stopped and was staring at them curiously.

He tried to keep his voice level because he had a lot of anger pent up. He had a lot he had to say to Jessica Bancroft, but he also had a lot to hide, and his churning emotions made him feel powerless and frustrated. He actually had to take a quivering breath before he stared into her brown eyes.

His heart melted at what he saw: there was confusion, and desire. She still had a thing for him, but she was hell-bent on living her little teenage dreams with Khaled.

"Why are you going out with him, Jess?" he asked hoarsely. "You still like me."

Jessica swallowed. "Because I want to. He's Khaled."

Clay shook his head. "This hero worship foolishness has gotten out of hand, don't you think?"

"Let me go, Clay," Jessica said, a small tremor in her voice.

Her father walked in as the two women stared at them silently. He also stood at the door silently.

"Ask him to sing for you, Jess," Clay said, releasing her hand. Ask him what the real color of his eyes are," he hissed, "and ask him to kindly return my poetry book that he stole from my apartment. He could at least have had the decency to return it after he used it to snatch you away from me, don't you think?"

Jessica gasped.

Clay sighed and started to walk away, but then turned to look at her again. "When you return, I won't be here. Have a good night."

"Clay," Jessica shook her head, "why won't you tell me why you hate Khaled so much?"

"Ask him," Clay said. "Ask David Green why is it that he tracked me down to Mount Faith, and why he is so interested in you? And whatever you do," he added over his shoulder, "don't sleep with him because I won't be around after that. I won't even try to understand why."

He walked to his room and closed the door quietly.

Jessica looked around and saw that she had an audience. Standing behind her father were her brothers, Adrian and Taj. Her mother and her sister were looking at her, concerned. She rubbed the hand that Clay had held onto. She wished that the floor could open up and swallow her. Did he have to confront her in front of her family like that? Then she remembered the repressed anger in his voice, and she felt a shiver dance along her spine.

Nobody said a word.

She swallowed nervously and then she heard a horn blow at the gate.

Her father was looking surprisingly calm. "You know, you should invite him to meet your parents. Blowing the horn for a girl at the gate is in such bad taste," he said simply.

Jessica had been ready to protest at whatever it is her parents or her brothers and sister were about to say but they didn't say a word. She wanted to scream, *say something!* but when their opinion mattered, they were unusually tight lipped. She had sort of expected her father to detain her as she walked on trembling legs toward the door.

Still, nobody commented. Her father opened the door wider for her to pass. Taj gave her a little tap on her shoulder, and Adrian was looking at the road fiercely, then he looked at her and gave her an understanding little nod.

She walked down to the gate and then looked back at the house. They had all come out on the veranda, and like silent statues, were staring at her as she got into the vehicle. She looked at David, barely seeing him as she looked back again, wondering why her once vocal, opinionated family had gotten so silent.

"What's wrong?" David asked, smiling.

"Er...nothing," she was feeling extremely uncomfortable. "Where are we going?"

"I thought we should have a night in tonight," David said, "A romantic dinner for two."

Jessica heard Clays voice in her head. *Whatever you do, don't sleep with him because I won't be around after that, I won't even try...*

Why didn't somebody stop her? Her usually protective father had held the door open and just let her pass with no comment. She was stewing so much at her family, her father especially, that she didn't even realized that they had reached the Blue Palm Apartment or that David had opened a door and was looking at her with a frown.

"I feel that something is not right with you," he said to her. She was acting as if she was in a trance.

Jessica shook her head. "I don't know. I am coming down with something I think."

David groaned. "I hope not. I wrote this really funny poem for you. Maybe it will cheer you up. It goes, *I am acid; you are alkaline, opposites in every way. The test tube is our world; the lab is our universe...*

Jessica remembered the first day she met Clay; she had asked him if he was going to do a poem about acids and alkaline in a test tube.

She looked at David as if he had two heads and walked like a zombie into the apartment. He couldn't be that dishonest; he just couldn't.

"When did you write that poem?" she asked.

He was cackling about it so hard that it took him a while to sober up.

"Last week," he said glibly.

Jessica swallowed, "I didn't know that you were interested in science."

"I am," David said, "very interested in scientific things, especially chemistry."

He poured out a glass of wine.

Jessica struggled to read the bottle. He knew she didn't drink alcohol. What was this, his attempt to make her drunk?

"To your chemistry and mine." He handed her a glass and tapped his to hers.

Jessica sniffed it, definitely alcohol. She took a sip and then coughed; the involuntary action made her spew the wine into his face.

He exclaimed. "What the hell!"

"Sorry," Jessica said insincerely. "I am not used to alcohol."

"My contacts." David got up hurriedly.

"Wait," Jessica said. He was cupping one eye.

"Look at me." She demanded.

David looked at her with a frown. "What's the matter?"

His eye was brown! Jessica shook her head and backed away toward the end of the settee. "Nothing. Maybe you should go and replace your contacts."

He nodded. When he got back his eyes were green again and he had changed his green shirt into a black silk one.

Jessica smiled. "That was quick."

David shrugged. "Where were we?"

"You were talking about our chemistry," Jessica reminded him.

"Yes." He nodded, looking doubtfully at her and the glass, as if he expected her to throw more wine into his eyes.

Jessica grinned at him. "I know, why don't you sing for me, like a private concert? You know, all this time you have been quoting poetry for me, so I know that you are a great songwriter. What could be more romantic than a private Khaled concert?"

David grinned. "Why not?" He picked up the remote and

turned on his stereo. His first album came on.

"No," Jessica said. "Live, do it for me live. Without music."

"No," David said looking uncomfortable, "I had a slight cold; I won't abuse my voice. I have a seventh album coming up."

He smiled at the romantically laid out table. "Let's eat."

Jessica toyed with the food in her plate, watching him cagily as he smiled at her. Was he all phony? Why didn't he want to sing for her? She knew that he didn't have a cold.

Her discomfort grew the longer dinner went on and then she blurted out the question that was bugging her more than anything else. "Why did you steal Clay's poetry book?"

David slowly and deliberately wiped his mouth. "Jessica, this is ridiculous. Is that what Clay told you? That I stole his book?"

Jessica nodded.

David got up. "You know, Clay has never liked me. He has always been jealous of me, but to go so low as to tell you that I stole his book." He shook his head. "I don't know what to say."

Jessica frowned. "You are the one who's lying, David. That poem about acid and alkaline was a joke between me and Clay the first day we met."

She got up. "I have to go."

David got up as well and held onto her hand. "But the night is not over sweet thing."

Jessica looked at him fiercely. "Let me go! You fake eyed, fake smile, fake poem quoting liar."

David shook her a bit. "Suppose I don't want to let you go. I like you Jessica. I think we have a connection."

"No we don't," Jessica shook her head and looked at him contemptuously. "Clay warned me about you weeks ago, but I decided to give you another chance. My gosh, was I stupid.

The thought kept churning in my mind that you were Khaled, my favorite artiste. I got caught up in my stupid dream, but it's only when you started quoting Clay's poems to me that I even started thinking of you differently. I am an imbecile."

David released her hand and snarled, "Maybe you are an imbecile. Who would choose a nobody like Clay over me? I am the famous Khaled." He looked at her with wrath in his eyes. "Get out! Don't expect me to drop you home though. It should be interesting to hear how you reach home in the dark, and in those shoes."

He went to the door and opened it, indicating with his head. "Bon voyage, man teaser."

Jessica went to the door and walked through. David slammed it after her. She jumped at the sound. Her eyes were teary when she stepped out in the walkway and looked out at the very dark night. She couldn't call home now; it would be too embarrassing.

A cough alerted her that she was not alone on the balcony. When she looked behind her, she saw her father and her brothers in the landing leaning up on the railing.

"Ready?" Her father asked.

She nodded numbly.

Chapter Sixteen

Jessica Bancroft hated to eat humble pie, and she was not looking forward to telling Clay that he was right. Khaled was not the person she thought he was; even his eyes weren't real.

Her father locked the front door behind her; he had not said a word of recrimination about her date. He, Taj, and Adrian had not even asked her why her date was so short, or what had really happened, or why she had come out of the apartment tearful and disoriented.

They had discussed cricket instead and then football—the international premier league. She had thought her father would have said something to her after he dropped off each of her brothers, but he didn't.

She headed for Clay's room and knocked. When she got no answer, she turned to her father in a panic. "Don't tell me he really left."

Her father nodded. "He is gone. I tried to convince him to

stay but he didn't want to be here when you got back."

"But," tears came to Jessica's eyes. "I am sorry. I am so sorry."

Her father nodded. "I know."

Jessica dropped to the floor. "I am such a fool." She put her face in her hands and sobbed. "I was duped. I thought David was genuine. I should have known. I didn't get the right vibe from him at first but I..."

"I know." Her father stooped beside her. He handed her a handkerchief, and she took it from him and sobbed into its folds.

Her dad sat on the floor with her. Through her tears, she realized that he was still in his work suit. He must have followed her after she got into the vehicle with David. He had loosened his tie and it hung around his neck untidily. He patted her hand. "It is not that bad kiddo. Life goes on. In a matter of weeks, you will move on."

Jessica sniffled, "Not from Clay. I really liked him and those poems...they were his. He wrote poems about me, except I really thought it was Khaled who wrote them."

"But you chose Khaled." her father said heavily. "Clay didn't look too happy when he left here."

"Where did he go?" Jessica lifted up her tear-stained face and looked at her father.

Bancroft shrugged. "I don't know. He said that he had two weeks of school left, gave us a polite speech thanking us for all we've done for him and then packed up his stuff and left."

Jessica sighed tremulously. "I am majorly stupid."

Bancroft kissed her on her forehead. "All of us have been through stuff like this, Jess. It's a part of life, a part of growing up."

"Why didn't you stop me?" Jessica asked, hiccupping.

Bancroft looked at her sideways. "Because you needed to

see for yourself, the kind of person you were dealing with. I must admit, when Clay insinuated that you might sleep with Khaled, I was surprised. My natural instinct was to lock you up in your room and throw away the key, but you are no longer my baby girl. I banked on the fact that you would have sense enough not to let it get that far with Khaled."

Jessica nodded. "I should have had sense enough not to go out with David 'Khaled' Green in the first place. Do you know that his eyes are not really green?"

Bancroft chuckled. "Doesn't surprise me."

"I am not letting my children listen to any popular music," Jessica said feelingly, "or watch movies, or get attached to any movie or TV stars, or singers."

Bancroft laughed. "Oh, Jess. You can't stop your children from making their own decisions about their likes and dislikes. You can guide them though."

Bancroft patted her hand after a while. "Feeling better?"

Jessica shook her head. "I am not sure I'll feel better again."

"Goodnight, my youngest." Bancroft said softly. "Try to get some sleep. My mother used to say things will look better in the morning."

Jessica got up stiffly and went into her room.

*****

Jessica waited in the lobby area of the science building the next day. This time she was waiting for Clay. Ironically, it was Ramon who found her in the lobby. Once more, she was trying to understand the weird science headlines that she saw on the magazine covers on the table.

Ramon sat beside her. "What's up?"

"I am waiting on Clay." Jessica glanced at him and then

back at the magazine.

"He doesn't want to talk to you, or about you," Ramon said. "I don't know what you did."

Jessica's lips trembled. "I was stupid."

Ramon nodded. "I figure this has something to do with Khaled."

"Yes, but I don't want an 'I told you' so speech," Jessica said hoarsely. "I just want to talk to Clay."

Ramon leaned back in the chair. "We just finished the final project. We barely slept last night. We were at the library until the wee hours of the morning."

"So that's where he was?" Jessica asked. "Is he gone back to Blue Palm Apartments?"

"Have no idea," Ramon said wearily.

Jessica got up. "I'll find him there."

"Wait, Jess," Ramon said. "Why don't you give him some space?"

"No," Jessica shook her head. "I have to tell him how stupid I was and apologize and hope that I can get us to be friends again."

Ramon rolled his eyes." He doesn't seem as if he's in the mood for that sort of thing. Give him some time."

Jessica walked off leaving Ramon mid protest.

*****

When she knocked on Clay's door at Blue Palm Apartments, she realized that his door was just beside Khaled's, and as if conjuring him up from her thoughts, Khaled exited his apartment. He looked back when he saw Jessica and pocketed his key.

He folded his arms. "If it isn't the ice princess?"

"If it isn't the fake green-eyed pop star."

Khaled chuckled. "All a part of the image darling."

He stared at her contemptuously. "Here to grovel to Clay?"

Jessica nodded. "Yes, he's ten times a better man than you are."

Khaled laughed. "Pity you didn't realize that before. You chose me, and that won't go down too well with him. Clay is particular like that. You are as good as dead to him now."

"I can't believe I liked you for so many years." Jessica turned back to Clay's door and knocked.

Khaled laughed. "I won't miss you as a fan. You see, I have too many to care about just one."

"Argh." Jessica shouted, "Clay. I know you are in there. I came to apologize."

The door swung open and Clay winced at the sunlight pouring in. He looked at Jessica. She was dressed in a blinding neon green top. He squinted at her, "Listen, Jess," he said hoarsely. "There is no need to apologize. Some people weren't meant to be together. You and I weren't. Have a nice life."

He closed the door in her face.

Jessica kicked the door in frustration. "But I grew up; I really grew up this time."

Khaled was leaning against the rail behind her. He laughed. "I would never slam the door in your face, pretty Jessica," he said mockingly. "Still sure that you don't want to take me up on my offer to explore our chemistry?"

Jessica hissed her teeth and walked toward her car. She had blown it with Clay. She glanced at the mocking features of Khaled as he headed for his car, which was parked near hers. She was completely over whatever had had her spellbound to him.

Chapter Seventeen

"**W**ant us to do something for Valentine's this year?" Jessica asked Ramon. As usual, the campus was awash with Valentine's decorations. Even the Business Center where they were currently sitting was advertising Valentine's specials for the budget conscious student, and they were playing love songs over the speakers.

Ramon shook his head. "Sorry, Jess. This year I have a killer date with Helen lined up."

"Oh, her," Jessica said, her voice lacking enthusiasm, "You two still going strong, huh?"

"Yes," Ramon grinned. "Something you would know if you weren't moping around the place. Last week we went to the circus in Santa Cruz. Remember? I invited you to come with us."

Jessica imitated a snoring sound.

Ramon laughed. "You know. You need to cheer up. You have been as lack luster as a wet blanket."

"How can I cheer up?" Jessica asked, "Clay won't talk to me. He ditched his phone; all I am getting is voicemail. I mean I made one mistake and this is how he behaves."

Ramon knew when to keep his mouth shut, and this was one of those times. Jessica was in free flow, and like he had done in the few weeks since Clay left Mount Faith, he listened without saying a word.

"I can't concentrate on my school work. I need to see him, at least to apologize."

"I thought you already did that." Ramon asked, slurping the drink in his cup noisily.

"Well, yes." Jessica drummed her fingers on the table. "I apologized, but he wasn't in the mood to hear. I realized too late that I loved him. People do get confused, you know."

Ramon shook his head, "Once more that Khaled fool destroyed something that you held dear. I have always known that there was a reason I hated him."

"Should I go to Kingston?" Jessica asked Ramon. "I mean, I should, shouldn't I?"

"And get the door slammed in your face there?" Ramon asked, "That's too long a journey to take just to get rejected."

"I should go on Valentine's day. That's two days from now. Why not?"

Ramon sighed. "Jess, listen to me, Clay was just a guy. You'll meet somebody like him again."

"No," Jessica said, "I won't. I think God sent him up here just for me."

"And I think you are crazy. Aren't you tired of the same reasoning? First, you said that Khaled was the person for you, and you didn't want anybody else; you killed us with that for years, and now that Khaled is out of the picture, it's back to Clay."

"And here is a new single just in time for Valentine's Day

from our very own alumnus, Khaled," sounded through the speakers before Jessica could react to Ramon.

She rolled her eyes, "I wonder what he is singing now, the self-centered prig! If I never hear a peep out of him again, it would be too soon."

Ramon shook his head, "I should get out of here because I don't want to hear him ever again." He got up.

"This song is your song, and you know who you are." It was Khaled's smoky voice.

Jessica rolled her eyes. "It must be for some clueless, idiotic girl. That soulless pig doesn't have a heart."

She got up with Ramon.

The cover of Smokey Robinson's song began. It had a light reggae beat. *Just to see her, Just to hold her in my arms again one more time...If I could feel her warm embrace, see her smiling face...*

Khaled sounded so good that for a moment Jessica closed her eyes and appreciated his voice. Such a pity he was such a doofus. Just then, she remembered Clay saying, "Just To See Her is my favorite song...Ask Khaled to sing for you... Ask David Green why he had to follow me to Mount Faith."

"Oh, my Gosh," she sat down hard on the bench that she had just vacated.

Ramon turned around. "What now?"

"Ramon Rodriguez. I think we are both idiots."

Ramon frowned. "What are you going on about?"

Jessica ran her fingers through her hair and then hit her head in her palm. "I can't believe this. I can't believe this...I can't believe this."

She was laughing and crying at the same time.

Ramon sat down. "Jess, if this is one of your dramatic episodes, welcome back. Such a pity that Khaled is the one who always seems to get these extreme emotions out of you."

"Yes, he is," Jessica nodded, her eyes shining. "Ramon, I can't believe this missed me, missed us? We have been hanging out with Khaled. He slept in my house, ate around my dining table. He played on my piano."

Ramon just stared at her as if she were insane.

"Clay is Khaled!" Jessica said, getting up. "Clay is Khaled!"

Ramon frowned. "Oh my god, she is having a nervous breakdown! Keep your voice down. Let's go visit your brother, Taj. He'll know what to do."

"I don't need psychiatric treatment," Jessica said, pinching Ramon. "Think about it Ramon, you are the bright scientific mind. When Clay came to Mount Faith, a few weeks after that Khaled announced his retirement. Why? Because Clay had retired! The voice had retired. The music had retired. David Green must only be a face."

Ramon was nodding, and then he clicked his fingers. "And both of them left Mount Faith at the same time, don't forget that. And Stewart, is David's friend. He must have set up the 'accident' so that Clay would be vulnerable when he got here. Maybe he wanted him to go back to Kingston as soon as it happened. When it was clear that Clay wasn't going to return to Kingston, he came here and dated you, knowing that Clay would leave if he pursued you, and you gave in..."

"Oh, boy," Jessica said deflated. "Ramon what am I going to do?"

"What are you going to do?" Ramon asked her urgently. "I would like to know, how they carried out this deception and whose idea it was? That means that 'Khaled' lip-syncs at concerts."

Jessica sighed.

"I think you should go to Clay," Ramon said. "The words of the song say, *there's nothing I wouldn't do just to see her again*... He said the song is dedicated to you."

"Suppose it's not for me," Jessica said doubtfully.

"Clay, left school so that the other guy could leave you alone," Ramon said gently. "I think that song is an invitation for you to go to him."

Jessica looked at her friend. "If you make me go to Kingston and get the door slammed in my face again..."

"You always said that Khaled wrote songs just for you or he was singing just for you. Here's your opportunity to test that theory. I could come with you if you want."

Jessica got up, "I am going alone. I want to be humiliated alone."

"Or reconciled without an audience." Ramon winked.

Chapter Eighteen

"It's V-Day," the announcer said on the radio. "If you don't have a Valentine, I can be your Valentine today, well, until my shift ends this morning." The announcer chuckled. "I'll kick things off with my favorite artiste, Khaled. He didn't stay retired for long. He released a single for a special girl, a cover of Smoky Robinson's, 'Just To See Her'."

Jessica turned up the radio. She was heading to Kingston and feeling very nervy. Her mother had told her to go. Her father had told her not to chase any man but he would leave her to make her own decision.

So here she was, with Clay's voice in her ear, spurring her on. He said he had to see her; at least, that was how she was reading the song. What if she was wrong and she was misreading things again like she had done so many times before?

She had a vague idea of where the studio was; it was in downtown Kingston, in the business district. The studio adjoined Ocean Towers and had a view of the sea. She drove through the semi-confusing streets and breathed a sigh of relief when she reached the building.

There was a sign on the ground floor with an iJam logo emblazoned on it. Jessica took a deep breath and walked up to the glass door and pressed the buzzer. A clicking sound indicated to her that the door was opened, and she walked into the lobby area. Her sneakers squeaked on the marble floor, and she wished that she had worn something a little bit more formal. She had no idea that iJam was in such an imposing looking building. There was a semi-circular desk with a security guard sitting around several monitors in what she assumed was the reception area.

"May I help you?" he asked before she could open her mouth.

"Yes...er...I am here to see Clay Reid."

"He's recording at the moment and he does not have any visitors on his list." The man, whose name tag read "Dudley", said to her pleasantly.

Jessica was confused. Did that mean that she wouldn't get to see Clay? She cleared her throat. "Could you tell him that Jessica Bancroft is out here in the lobby waiting to see him?"

The security guard frowned. "I am sorry Miss Bancroft, but I am not allowed to interrupt Mr. Reid when he is in the studio."

"When does he come out of the studio?" Jessica asked frantically. This was like the door slamming in her face again.

"I can't give you that information," The security guard said. "I am sorry."

Jessica nodded. She took out her cell phone and dialed Clay's number again. As usual, it went to voicemail. She was so close, and yet so far.

She looked around the lobby. There was a bank of chairs

in a waiting area. "Tell Clay, when he is free, that Jessica is here," she said to the security guard, heading for the chairs. What a way to spend Valentine's Day. She was hoping for a different outcome when she set out this morning.

She looked around at the paintings on the wall. Most of them were abstracts. The whole lobby was decorated in a chrome plus glass look, and the paintings provided the only splash of color. She looked at her watch. It was ten o'clock. She picked up one of the several magazines on the table and then put it back down. She was too keyed up to read. She just wanted to see Clay.

She tapped her foot on the floor and then picked up the magazine again. The security guard was looking at her with a frown between his brows.

At ten thirty-five, the door made a ping sound, and she looked up and saw Neil Reid stepping through the door. He had a briefcase in hand, and he looked professional in his dark suit. She had always thought that a music executive was more casual in his dress, and that the place would be buzzing with artistes or something.

"Mr. Reid." She got up hurriedly.

Neil stopped and looked at her, shocked. "Jessica Bancroft?"

He smiled, but his eyes looked shifty. "What brings you here to our neck of the woods?"

"I came to see Clay." Jessica pushed her hand in her jeans pocket.

"Ah," Neil said. "Please join me in my office." They walked up a flight of stairs that also had the chrome and glass theme, and entered an office space that had windows overlooking the harbor.

Jessica couldn't appreciate the view though. She was tensing up for further rejection.

"Can I see Clay?" she asked. "The guy at the desk downstairs said that he would be unavailable all day."

"Have a seat," Neil said, without answering her. He indicated to a group of sofas that were in front of a huge television screen. "Do you want a drink, or something to eat? We have everything."

"No, thanks," Jessica replied, sitting down. Neil was not reaching for the phone or making any moves to get Clay, and Jessica felt nervous.

"It is my understanding that you chose David over Clay in some romantic tug of war that you guys had," Neil said, caressing his goatee.

"It's not a matter of choosing," Jessica said, feeling unable to defend herself. She had chosen David and what a fool's gold he had turned out to be.

Neil sighed. "You hurt Clay, and I think you both should go your separate ways and forget each other."

"But his latest song was a message to me," Jessica said desperately, her hopes dashed with every word Neil Reid spoke.

He looked at her and guffawed. "What do you mean his latest song?"

"Just to see her," Jessica said, almost weakly. "The announcer on the radio said that it was dedicated to," she took in a deep breath, "a special girl."

Neil was looking at her, concerned. "I thought you said that you were here to see Clay."

"I am," Jessica said uncertainly. "Isn't he the one who sings?"

"Who told you that?" Neil was frowning now.

"Nobody told me," Jessica said. "I know both Clay and David, and there is no way that David is a singer or even poetic. He is as fake as..."

Neil sat back in his chair. "What a conclusion to draw?"

"But it's true, isn't it?" Jessica asked earnestly.

"Have you shared this with anyone?" Neil asked seriously. He was looking at her so intensely that Jessica stammered when she answered.

"No...no...er...well, yes. I shared it with my friend Ramon."

Neil sighed. "Clay is driving himself to do this seventh album in a short time span so that he can see you and reveal all," Neil confessed. "He has been miserable and yes, he dedicated that song to you."

"I knew it," Jessica said, a feeling of relief almost swamping her. "Can I see him?"

Neil picked up the phone. "Why not? He'd have come to see you anyway."

"Jessica is here," he said abruptly into the phone.

A few moments after that she heard running down the hallway and then Clay stood at the doorway. She was suddenly feeling nervy and unsure of herself, but Clay saw her and his face lit up. "I knew you'd come." He came further into the room and grabbed her into a bear hug. She hugged him back tightly too.

"Come, let's go talk in my office." He glanced at his uncle, who had a querying look in his eyes.

Neil fanned him on. "Yes, you can tell her. She already figured it out anyway. But young lady," Neil said, looking at Jessica, "this information cannot go out to the public until the studio wants it to. It is our information to reveal."

*****

Clay pulled her into the office that was beside his uncle's and closed the door. He kissed her hard as soon as she opened her mouth to speak. "I missed you," he said huskily. "I really did. It was like agony, and when I did the cover, I wondered if you would get the message I was sending."

Jessica looked into his dark brown eyes and saw the sincerity and the warmth there.

"I had no idea that you were really Khaled."

"Jess, I gave you so many clues in our conversations. I was bound by a stupid contract. I still am bound not to talk about our arrangement, but my uncle said I could give you one last clue, so I did with that song, and you finally figured it out."

He hugged her to him again.

Jessica nuzzled her face into his shirt. "I am so happy that I came."

Clay laughed. "Me too. My uncle and I made a deal. If you came to visit me, then I could tell you."

"But he tried to send me away," Jessica said, appalled.

"He doesn't want you to know." Clay pulled her over to his settees. His were red; his uncle's were black. "He doesn't want anybody to know. So where do I begin?" they snuggled together.

"At the beginning. Who is David Green?" Jessica asked.

"He is my uncle's son."

"What?" Jessica asked. "Are you serious?"

"Yes." Clay kissed her and held her even closer to him. "Eight years ago, my uncle discovered that he had a love child with a woman of... er... questionable reputation. The child, David Green, came to seek him out when he was twenty-two. He was broke and in desperate need of help, and his mother had just died. She had told him a list of men who possibly could be his father. My uncle was the last name on the list.

When David came by my uncle had a dilemma on his hands. He didn't want anybody knowing that David was his, but he felt an obligation to help him to do something useful. Unfortunately, David wasn't skilled in anything, and though he fancied himself a singer, he couldn't sing. He was becoming a nuisance for my uncle and his business associates, so my uncle hatched a plan to get David productive.

I could sing, but I hated the limelight, so my uncle came up with the brilliant idea of creating a composite of the perfect artiste. David would be the face of the artiste and I, the voice. David would get to do all the touring and interviews, and I would produce the songs and write the lyrics. That artiste was called 'Khaled'. Believe you me, we had no idea that the Khaled brand would have exploded so big."

Jessica whispered. "Oh, Clay. I should have known. The lyrics and the music were all you."

Clay nodded. "We signed a seven album contract, and there is a clause that nobody could reveal the real identity of Khaled in the seven years."

"So you couldn't tell me when you were at Mount Faith," Jessica said.

"No, not even when I saw that you were crying over my retirement." Clay shook his head. "I wanted to tell you then. I wanted to tell you so many times. I came this close." He kissed her on the forehead.

"Ramon said that David and Stewart are friends."

"Yes, they are, and Stewart trying to blind me wasn't an accident. David is incredibly jealous of me and very addicted to his life as a superstar," Clay said, "so when I retired at six albums he panicked, announced his retirement too, and followed me to Mount Faith. He sent Stewart first to do something to make me vulnerable, so that I would return to Kingston. The science experiment was an opportunity."

"So all along I had the 'hots' for the right person." Jessica sighed. "I am going to laugh at this sometime far into the future, but for now I feel like an idiot for choosing a phony over you. I am so sorry, Clay."

"You are here now, and that's all that matters." Clay entangled his fingers with hers.

Epilogue

It was the most well attended anniversary party the Bancrofts had ever put on. Ryan and Celeste were celebrating thirty years together as man and wife.

This year the family had swollen in number, and so many friends wanted to attend that the president's ballroom was the chosen venue. Even the weather was smiling on them. The theme was classic 80's, and the ballroom was decorated in pale blue and gold, their wedding colors.

The Bancroft children filed in with their spouses and children and were directed to sit at a special table, in order of age.

"I am usually not at a loss for words," Ryan Bancroft said when it was his time to make a toast, "but thirty years is a lot of years to be with the same bossy woman. I find myself not knowing where to start." There were chuckles from the more than two hundred people there. "I may be the president at work, but when I am home, I know that I have a co-president, and her name is Celeste.

Tonight, Celeste and I are happy for the blessing of our children, all of them, and we are happy for their spouses. Adrian and Kylie have made us grandparents, and we are happy for the other generation, and we know that there will be more to come." He raised his glass. "Tonight we have with us Clay Reid. He will sing, for our first dance, the song 'Stand By Me'. I must tell you that this song was playing the night I nervously approached Celeste and asked her for a date in the school cafeteria, no less.

Before she answered and said yes, she asked me if I knew that this song was based on Psalm 46. I stammered and said 'yes'. Then she had the audacity to ask me to repeat the first three verses of Psalm 46." The audience chuckled. "Luckily, the Lord brought the text to my mind, and I repeated it. For those of you not too familiar with it, it says: 'God is our refuge and strength, an ever-present help in trouble. Therefore we will not fear, though the earth give way and the mountains fall into the heart of the sea, though its waters roar and foam and the mountains quake with their surging.'"

Celeste and I have been through many troubling situations over the years, but we have always borne in mind who is our present help. That was our wedding song, by the way, and today it is still a favorite of ours."

I thank God for her, and I thank God for the children, and our niece, and nephew and all their partners: Taj and Natasha, Micah and Charlene, Adrian and Cathy, Marcus and Deidra, Kylie and Gareth, Vanley and Davia, Arnella and Alric, and Jessica and Clay. May he bless your unions also. Remember that when you are in trouble you should seek 'Him who is able to keep you from falling'."

He turned to the children and raised his glass. Jessica was sitting at the piano on the stage to accompany Clay. He was singing as himself in front of an audience for the first time. They all raised their glasses to cheer Celeste and Ryan Bancroft.

Then Jessica started playing the song "Stand By Me" while Celeste and Ryan danced the first dance and their children joined them on the dance floor.

THE END

Brenda Barrett is proud to introduce her gripping new series,
THE NEW SONG SERIES.

Welcome to six brand new titles set in the city of Montego Bay
that unfold to reveal the stories of six men, their loves,
their trials and their triumphs
and the women that their hearts beat for.

Step into the world of The New Song Band with
GOING SOLO

Going Solo

"She's back!" Carson's office door flew open and his daughter rushed in, her eyes wide and looked overly excited. "I passed her when I was heading into the mini mart and she didn't even know that it was me."

Carson was busy signing off on invoices, a task he took great pleasure in, as he had left the more greasy hard work to his employees and was enjoying the business side of things just as Xavier had said he would.

"Who is back?" he asked his daughter absentmindedly. It was the beginning of summer and he was already wondering what to do with his hyperactive twelve-year-old daughter. She had already run through the five books that he bought her last week, and summer school was not about to start until a month's time.

"The female who had me," Mia answered primly.

Carson stopped writing and looked at his daughter properly for the first time. The little spattering of freckles she had on her nose seemed to merge into one as he struggled to get her face in focus. The pen he was using clattered onto the table, and he frowned.

"Stop joking around. That is not funny."

Mia walked toward his desk, her floral summer dress swishing around her legs. She stopped and jutted one foot forward, looking at him defiantly.

"I know it's her." She folded her arms in a defensive pose. "She doesn't look much different from her pictures, except that her hair is shorter. She came out of the car she was driving and asked Emril if CarBell Mechanics was run by one Carson Bell, and Emril said yes. And then the lady who had me, took in a long breath and then got back into her car.

I could see her hand trembling from where I stood, and she looked shaken up. She looked human, unlike the half-alien I was imagining."

Carson drummed his fingers on the table and then said softly, "She is human, Mia, and you can say her name, you know. Her name is Alice."

"Alice." Mia sneered and then slumped, all her bravado leaving her lifeless. "What are we going to do about her?"

"We are going to do nothing," Carson said simply. His heart was beating heavily though, and he had a breathless feeling. If it was really Alice and not some doppelganger, that would make it exactly ten years since she left, ten years since she walked out on him leaving him holding their toddler, Mia.

Today was June 10. The first three years he had been glad to see the back of her, but for the last couple of years or so he had been yearning for answers and some closure. He didn't know if he would understand her reasons, but he certainly wanted a few questions cleared up.

"I think we should ignore her," Mia said. "If she comes here, then we slam the door in her face."

"Mia," Carson looked at her sternly, "I don't want you talking like that about your mom." He looked at Mia's spirited piquant face and at the sparks that were flying behind her eyes, and he saw a little bit of Alice in her face, especially now that she was angry.

"She's not my mom. She's a mother," Mia said slowly and deliberately. "She's just a biological mother. She's the equivalent of a sperm donor father who just..."

"Enough," Carson said to his daughter, watching as she bristled with indignation.

"Obviously, Mia, I can't tell you how to feel about Alice, but she is still your mother." He paused. He didn't even know how he felt about Alice. If you looked too closely at his emotions, they wouldn't pass muster either.

"Aunt Ruby said that she was a heartless person who doesn't deserve us and that..."

"Ruby shouldn't be telling you anything about Alice. She barely knew her." Carson cut in before Mia could continue. He knew that behind all the bravado and sneering was a little girl who longed to have a female figure in her life. He would have to have a talk with Ruby, Ian's wife, or ask Ian to talk to Ruby later at band practice that night. She shouldn't be spreading poison to an impressionable girl about her own mother, even if that mother deserved it.

He looked over the invoices on his desk and rested back in his chair. The briskness with which he had been tackling the papers on his desk was now gone. He felt a sense of doom and helplessness that he had not started the day with, and only because Alice was back.

He looked at Mia, who was chewing her fingernails, devouring them as if they were food. It was a habit he had spent the last six months trying to get her to quit.

"I am going to band practice," he said to her. "Want to come?"

"No," Mia said, "I want to talk."

"Okay," he said, packing up the papers that were strewn across his desk. "What do you want to talk about?"

He glanced at the clock. Every Wednesday at five, they had band practice upstairs his building. He had a huge warehouse up there, and one of the first things he and the guys had done was create a space for the band in the vast expanse. They had put up some dry walls to partition the space where they practiced and painted it into a bright yellow. They added a bathroom, a kitchenette, and a small room with two single beds, just in case anybody needed to crash there. As time went by, someone had carried a television so that they didn't miss the news or sports, and more and more odds and ends had found themselves up there. Last year they added a pool table. They even had a small office, a notice board, and a sound proof room for recording.

His mechanic shop and auto parts store was at a convenient location near down town Montego Bay for all the band members to stop by on their way from work. Sometimes they stopped by just to hang out. The space had its own entrance, and everybody had keys.

"I want to talk about her," Mia said softly, after a long pause that almost made him forget that he had asked the question.

Carson sighed, "Mia can we talk about her when we go home? I'll tuck you up in bed, and I will answer all the questions I possibly can."

"Promise," Mia said, twirling her ponytail.

"Promise." He came around the desk and hugged her to him. She burrowed her face in the front of his shirt.

"I love you, Daddy."

"I love you too, Muffin. Come upstairs and get me if you need anything." He watched her as she slowly walked out of the office. Her slim frame was hovering between that of a child and a teenager. He would soon have to go bra shopping with her and discuss changes in her body, and boys, and all of the things that he didn't think he would have to tackle alone at this stage of her life, especially since she had a mother who was alive.

He shook his head and watched as she arched her neck toward him, her heart shaped face looked sad. "Have a good practice, Daddy." Sorrow and loneliness dripped off every word. Guilt, raw and unadulterated, gripped him. He felt as if he was abandoning her just by going upstairs. He tampered down that feeling. Mia knew she would always have him around, and though his natural inclination was to cocoon and shield her, he wanted her to grow up to be an independent woman, not clingy and needy. It was a tough balance to strike because sometimes he found himself wanting to be overprotective.

"I am just going to be upstairs," he said softly. "I am not going anywhere. After that we will go home. Don't eat any junk food at the Mart, okay. I am going to fix us dinner when we get home."

She walked through the door and closed it softly. His confident Muffin was now acting like an abandoned child.

Alice, oh, Alice. Why did you leave, and why are you back? How long would she stay this time? And why was she even here? His mind churned up question after question.

He got up from the desk and closed the drawers, pocketed the key, and headed toward the stairs in the middle of the building, up to brand practice, the only thing that kept him sane through the years...

OTHER BOOKS BY BRENDA BARRETT

Love Triangle Series

Love Triangle: Three Sides To The Story - George, the husband, Marie, the wife and Karen-the mistress. They all get to tell their side of the story.

Love Triangle: After The End -Torn between two lovers. Colleen married her high school sweetheart, Isaiah, hoping that they would live happily ever after but life intruded and Isaiah disappeared at sea. She found work with the rich and handsome, Enrique Lopez, as a housekeeper and realized that she couldn't keep him at arms length...

Love Triangle: On The Rebound - For Better or Worse, Brandon vowed to stay with Ashley, but when worse got too much he moved out and met Nadine. For the first time in years he felt happy, but then Ashley remembered her wedding vows...

New Song Series

Going Solo (New Song Series-Book 1) - Carson Bell, had a lovely voice, a heart of gold, and was no slouch in the looks department. So why did Alice abandon him and their daughter? What did she want after ten years of silence?

Duet on Fire (New Song Series-Book 2) - Ian and Ruby had problems trying to conceive a child. If that wasn't enough, her ex-lover the current pastor of their church wants her back...

Tangled Chords (New Song Series-Book 3) - Xavier Bell, the poor, ugly duckling has made it rich and his looks have been incredibly improved too. Farrah Knight, hotel heiress had cruelly rejected him in the past but now she needed help. Could Xavier forgive and forget?

Broken Harmony (New Song Series-Book 4) - Aaron Lee, wanted the top job in his family company but he had a moral clause to consider just when Alka, his married ex-girlfriend walks back into his life.

A Past Refrain (New Song Series-Book 5) - Jayce had issues with forgetting Haley Greenwald even though he had a new woman in his life. Will he ever be able to shake his love for Haley?

Perfect Melody (New Song Series-Book 6) - Logan Moore had the perfect wife, Melody but his secretary Sabrina was hell bent on breaking up the family. Sabrina wanted Logan whatever the cost and she had a secret about Melody, that could shatter Melody's image to everyone.

The Bancroft Family Series

Homely Girl (The Bancrofts-Book 0) - April and Taj were opposites in so many ways. He was the cute, athletic boy that everybody wanted to be friends with. She was the overweight, shy, and withdrawn girl. Do April and Taj have a love that can last a lifetime? Or will time and separate paths rip them apart?

Saving Face (The Bancrofts-Book 1) - Mount Faith University drama begins with a dead president and several suspects including the president in waiting Ryan Bancroft.

Tattered Tiara (The Bancrofts-Book 2) - Micah Bancroft is targeted by femme fatale Deidra Durkheim. There are also several rape cases to be solved.

Private Dancer (The Bancrofts-Book 3) - Adrian Bancroft was gutted when he returned to Jamaica and found out that his first and only love Cathy Taylor was a stripper and was literally owned by the menacing drug lord, Nanjo Jones.

Goodbye Lonely (The Bancrofts-Book 4) - Kylie Bancroft was shy and had to resort to going to confidence classes. How could she win the love of Gareth Beecher, her faculty adviser, a man with a jealous ex-wife in his past and a current mystery surrounding a hand found in his garden?

Practice Run (The Bancrofts Book 5) - Marcus Bancroft had many reasons to avoid Mount Faith but Deidra Durkheim was not one of them. Unfortunately, on one of his visits he was the victim of a deliberate hit and run.

Sense of Rumor (The Bancrofts-Book 6) - Arnella Bancroft was the wild, passionate Bancroft, the creative loner who didn't mind living dangerously; but when a terrible thing happened to her at her friend Tracy's party, it changed her. She found that courting rumors can be devastating and that only the truth could set her free.

A Younger Man (The Bancrofts- Book 7) - Pastor Vanley

Bancroft loved Anita Parkinson despite their fifteen-year age gap, but Anita had a secret, one that she could not reveal to Vanley. To tell him would change his feelings toward her, or force him to give up the ministry that he loved so much.

Just To See Her (The Bancrofts- Book 8) - Jessica Bancroft had the opportunity to meet her fantasy guy Khaled, he was finally coming to Mount Faith but she had feelings for Clay Reid, a guy who had all the qualities she was looking for. Who would she choose and what about the weird fascination Khaled had for Clay?

The Three Rivers Series

Private Sins (Three Rivers Series-Book 1) - Kelly, the first lady at Three Rivers Church was pregnant for the first elder of her church. Could she keep the secret from her husband and pretend that all was well?

Loving Mr. Wright (Three Rivers Series-Book 2) - Erica saw one last opportunity to ditch her single life when Caleb Wright appeared in her town. He was perfect for her, but what was he hiding?

Unholy Matrimony (Three Rivers Series-Book 3) - Phoebe had a problem, she was poor and unhappy. Her solution to marry a rich man was derailed along the way with her feelings for Charles Black, the poor guy next door.

If It Ain't Broke (Three Rivers Series-Book 4) - Chris Donahue wanted a place in his child's life. Pinky Black just wanted his love. She also wanted him to forget his obsession with Kelly and love her. That shouldn't be so hard? Should it?

The Preacher And The Prostitute - Prostitution and the clergy don't mix. Tell that to ex-prostitute, Maribel, who finds herself in love with the Pastor at her church. Can an ex-prostitute and a pastor have a future together?

New Beginnings - Inner city girl Geneva was offered an opportunity of a lifetime when she found out that her 'real' father was a very wealthy man. Her decision to live up-town meant that she had to leave Froggie, her 'ghetto don,' behind. She also found herself battling with her stepmother and battling her emotions for Justin, a suave up-towner.

Full Circle - After graduating from university, Diana wanted to return to Jamaica to find her siblings. What she didn't foresee was that she would meet Robert Cassidy and that both their pasts would be intertwined, and that disturbing questions would pop up about their parentage, just when they were getting close.

Historical Fiction/Romance

The Empty Hammock - Workaholic, Ana Mendez, fell asleep in a hammock and woke up in the year 1494. It was the time of the Tainos, a time when life seemed simpler, but Ana knew that all of that was about to change.

The Pull Of Freedom - Even in bondage the people, freshly arrived from Africa, considered themselves free. Led by Nanny and Cudjoe the slaves escaped the Simmonds' plantation and went in different directions to forge their destiny in the new country called Jamaica.

Jamaican Comedy (Material contains Jamaican dialect)

Di Taxi Ride And Other Stories - Di Taxi Ride and Other Stories is a collection of twelve witty and fast paced short stories. Each story tells of a unique slice of Jamaican life.

CPSIA information can be obtained at www.ICGtesting.com
Printed in the USA
LVOW06s2134260715

447744LV00008B/63/P